# Spanish Gold Fever

Gold discovered out in California excites young Dan Bartlett, but life as a '49er isn't what he expected. Penniless, hungry and still innocent of life, he takes work holding a few horses, and when his new partner Tom Hodges yells at him to get in the saddle and ride, he naturally does as he's told.

Then Dan realizes that they are riding stolen stock and, believing the law is behind them, they head into Nevada Territory, where Hodges remembers having seen a little valley, a place where they can start a ranch. But en route for the valley, they come across an abandoned gold mine. It doesn't matter it isn't California gold; any gold draws interest – and when Dan finds himself looking into the barrel of a Colt .45 is when he really begins to grow up.

# Spanish Gold Fever

Bill Sheehy

A Black Horse Western

ROBERT HALE

ISBN 978-0-7198-2453-1

The Crowood Press
The Stable Block
Crowood Lane
Ramsbury
Marlborough
Wiltshire SN8 2HR

www.bhwesterns.com

Robert Hale is an imprint
of The Crowood Press

Typeset by
Derek Doyle & Associates, Shaw Heath

Printed and bound in Great Britain by
CPI Group (UK) Ltd, Croydon, CR0 4YY

# CHAPTER 1

Gold Ridge wasn't anything like the newspapers had said it would be. Daniel Bartlett might have been, as they say, wet behind the ears, but he was smart enough to see that it had all been a pack of lies. Gold, free for the taking, the newspaper had said. All a fella had to do was pick it up. The evidence before the young man said different. If there was so much gold that a fella could simply pick it up out of the creek, then why were there so many men looking like bums? Hungry bums, at that, and he knew about being a hungry bum because that's what he was; a cold, hungry twenty-year-old fool.

Was it only six months ago that he'd left Pa's farm? Yep, with the whole world to discover and a dream of gold in his head, he'd ridden old Bess out of the yard, looking back to give the family a smile and a final wave. Pa had already turned and was heading out to finish planting the north section.

He'd felt good sitting up on Bess's broad back, homespun-covered legs dangling. With twenty Liberty head gold coins, his pa's six-shot pepperbox pistol and California in his sights, he was the happiest he'd ever been. Well, the twenty dollars hadn't lasted long and Bess hadn't made it much further, but he'd arrived at the gold fields. A little older, not much wiser and a lot hungrier.

'That's it, boy,' said Marcus Allen, lifting the reins, ready to gee up the bullocks. 'This is what you're after, ain't it? The California gold country?' The older man's lips lifted in his sneering humourless smile. Bartlett grimaced at the black teeth behind the smile.

'Yeah, I guess so.'

'Wal, get your lazy butt off the wagon so I can go on. I still gotta a few miles before I'm done travelling.'

It was on the fourth or fifth morning on the trail that Bartlett had come awake to find old Bess unable to get up from where she lay. Sometime during the night it had started to rain, a steady dripping shower that left him shivering in his bedding.

Leaving Bess behind, he'd tied the soggy blankets into a roll and started walking. Wasn't anything he could do for the animal, but he felt bad about forsaking her. Maybe she'd be able to rest up and be of some use to someone else. Maybe.

The next stage of his trip west was with a wagon train. He hired on to help with the stock, taking his food as payment. That lasted until the train reached Fort Hall. A few of the wagons broke off to go southwest while the rest went on northwest into Oregon. Bartlett was heading for California.

Travelling along what someone called the Mormon Trail would, he was told, take him across the Sierra Nevada Mountains and right smack-dab in the middle of the Gold Rush. That's when he hired on with Allen.

Marcus Allen's wagon, pulled by a team of oxen, was

loaded down with supplies ordered by the owner of a general store in Sacramento. Putting up with the grumbling old man was part of the price the young man had to pay. With the magic of words like Sacramento, gold and California ringing in his ears, young Danny held his silence.

Until they came to a halt at Gold Ridge.

'I'm darn glad we got here,' Daniel Bartlett said, pulling his canvas-covered bedroll out from behind the wagon seat. 'And damn glad I can finally get shut of you and your grouching. I do thank you, but if I had to ride one more mile listening to you complain, I swear, I'd end up shoving my boot down your throat.'

Jumping down, he felt his boots sink in the mud of the roadway.

Laughing like he'd heard the biggest joke ever, Allen cracked his long black whip over the head of the lead ox. He was still laughing as the wagon moved on down between the tents making up the town.

'Wal, now, sonny, I guess you really told him, didn't you,' Bartlett heard a soft voice speak behind him.

'I saw you looking around and it's plain as the nose on your face, you just got over a bad case of gold fever.' The man talking was leaning against a post with both hands sunk deep in the pockets of a heavy sheepskin coat. He might have been smiling. His comments sounded like he was. Bartlett couldn't tell. The stranger's mouth was hidden by a dirty cloud of beard.

'Yep,' the man went on, 'I seen it time and again, come out here to get rich and take a pocket full of the yellow stuff home to that sweet little girl down in town. Uh huh, yes sirree, that's the idea. Until you come over that bunch

7

a mountains back yonder and see it for what it is. Well, don't go feeling so bad. You aren't the first and likely won't be the last. Hells fire, I'm one myself. Where you from anyway?' he asked, then not giving Bartlett a chance to answer, nodded. 'Naw, that doesn't matter none. You're young and whatever you been won't be anything like whatever you're going to be. Uh huh, that's the way it is. Now me, well, I've been dab near everywhere. And came back, too. What I discovered is there ain't no pockets of gold to be had unless you're planning on sweating for it. What, you haven't anything to say? Cat got your tongue?'

Bartlett shook his head. 'Nope. I'm hungry enough any cat get close I'd end up taking a bite of it. You think there's any place a fella could get a meal and maybe wash dishes to pay for it?'

'Ain't that the way of it?' the stranger laughed. 'You come over the mountain back yonder without two coins to rub together, thinking you might end up with enough gold to make it all worthwhile. Son, I got to tell it, you ain't going to find no dishes to wash in this camp. No, sir. Look around and tell me you're not just like most of the gents you see. So, you miss a few meals. Won't do any harm. Might make your thinking a bit quicker. And you got some thinking to do. Like where are you going to find that gold treasure you've been thinking about. Uh huh. That's a right nice question, wouldn't you say?'

Bartlett was sure everyone near him could hear his stomach growl.

'You don't seem to be a lot of help," he said, his head still moving as he continued to see what there was to see. 'I reckon maybe I'll have to go looking, see what's around, what others are doing. There's got to be something I can do to make a few dollars, enough to get a meal or two anyhow.'

'Now, that's the ticket. Yes, siree, Boy. But let's look at it. What're you willing to do to earn those meals? You're young-looking and I'd figure you've done your share of following along behind a plough pulled by some sorry old mule. Ain't any of that kind of work here. No, sir. Now if you weren't too particular I expect a man could make a little poke if he really wanted to.'

'Grandpa, the way my stomach's talking, I'd say there wasn't much I couldn't do to earn that poke you mentioned. Where do I sign up?'

The bearded man pushed himself away from the post and waved Bartlett to follow. 'C'mon, let's us go talk a bit. I got a camp set up and unless some jackass has robbed me, I got enough side meat and coffee to make a meal. By the way, I'm not so old as to be your grandpa and my name's Hodges, Thomas J. Hodges. You can call me Hodges.'

'My name's Daniel Bartlett. Most times I'm called Danny.'

'Danny it is, then. C'mon.'

The strips of bacon the older man laid out in the black iron fry pan were mostly fat, Danny saw, but that didn't stop his mouth from watering from the smell of them cooking. After wiping the blade on a pants leg, Hodges used his belt knife to separate four or five of the bigger pieces. Leaving a couple for himself, he passed the fry pan handle over to the youngster.

'You wouldn't be carrying any kind of weapon, would you?' he asked, watching Bartlett wolf down the first strip without wasting time chewing.

'Well, yes sir, Mr Hodges, I do. I got the pistol my pa gave me when I left out. Why?' he asked, reaching for a second thick slice of the fatty meat.

The man started to answer but stopped when three men came out of the brush to stand across the fire.

'Dammit, Hodges. You was gonna meet us down at the bridge and here you are, feeding your face and talking with some stranger.'

'Now, Matlow, this here's my new partner. Didn't you say you were looking for an extra hand or two? Well, hells fire, now with him you got enough, don't you?'

Danny didn't let the newcomers stop his eating but continued to chew while looking the men over. The one the old man called Matlow was the biggest of the three, his shoulders square under a long black waterproofed canvas coat. The coat wasn't buttoned and Bartlett could see the man had a wide leather belt around his waist holding a holstered revolver. The tops of his canvas pants tucked into the stovepipe tops of leather dog-eared boots. His face was partially hidden by the floppy brim of his black felt high-crowned hat. The part Bartlett could see was unsmiling and hard-looking.

Danny couldn't take his eyes off the man standing next to the big one. He'd never seen a man who looked like that. Somehow he looked as if he'd been put together wrong. This one wasn't wearing a hat and his head was hairless. Bigger than normal ears stuck out from the sides of his bald head. His nose lay almost flat above a pair of fat lips. Danny figured the nose had been broken, probably more than once. The man's arms were long, and his huge hands with long fingers hung almost to his knees. The youngster knew he was staring and when he saw the misshapen man staring back, he blanched and quickly shifted his gaze elsewhere.

'What you looking at, boy?' the man snarled.

'Leave it, Biles,' Matlow cut in curtly. 'What're you trying to pull, Hodges?' he snarled. 'He ain't nothing by a kid. I'm looking for men, not snot-nosed kids.'

Danny saw the third man had stopped and was standing off to one side a little. This one was slender (Pa would have said he was skinny), and he was flashier dressed than his friends. The pants he wore were of a kind the former farm boy had never seen before, some kind of leather, all tight from the waist to his knees then flaring out over his pointy-toed boots. Silver bangles had been sewn down the outside seam of the pants. A short brocaded vest over his shirt stopped at the man's waist, just above a narrow gun belt that held a pair of holstered pistols.

'Uh, ya,' said Hodges quietly, agreeing with Matlow, 'he's young. But very hungry. That means he can be counted on to do what needs done. Uh huh, and he's got his own pistol, too. Look, Matlow, do you want a bunch who'll do what they should or do you simply want bodies? Hell's fire, the town is full of them kind.'

Matlow stood staring at Bartlett for a long moment.

'OK. There isn't a lot of time to argue. You know where to be and when. Make sure you're both there. C'mon, you two,' the big man said, turning to head down toward town.

Danny finished the last piece of bacon and wiped his hands on his pants leg.

'OK. It looks like you got me some work. And I do thank you, Mr Hodges, but what exactly will I be doing

11

that I'll need Pa's pistol for?'

'Well, sonny, that there's Ned Matlow. He's the one we're working with now. He's put together a bunch of men to look out for a stagecoach that's going to make a run down to Sacramento. It'll be carrying a load of gold from the diggings back up yonder. There's been a few hold-ups and this time it'll be guarded heavier than before.'

'I don't know that I'd trust that fella that was standing there, the ugly one.'

Hodges chuckled. 'Yeah, he's a strange one, all right. That's Johnny Biles and a word of warning; he's damn quick with that pistol he carries. Quick to use it. It won't do to rile him.'

'I suppose I can't turn down any work that comes along, but there's something about those men I'm not feeling good about. What exactly will we be doing, Mr Hodges?'

'Don't worry, I'll be there to tell you how it goes. And don't be calling me mister. Just plain Hodges, will do. Or Tom, if you'd rather.'

# CHAPTER 2

After cleaning the fry pan and banking the little campfire, Hodges led Danny back down to the mining camp. Out of habit, Danny had swung his bedroll over a shoulder before following the older man. Hodges, he noticed, didn't bother with his belongings, simply walked away.

Old man Allen had called it Gold Ridge, but it certainly didn't look big enough to even have a name. Mostly it was just two rows of buildings that were no more than big canvas tents sitting on top of walls of rough-sawn boards. The dozen or so businesses lining both sides of the mud-choked roadway were mostly gambling halls or saloons.

'Where are we going to meet up with this stagecoach?' he asked, not seeing anything that looked like a stage-coach.

Hodges didn't respond but kept walking. Passing the last of the tent buildings, he lifted his chin, pointing to the twin ruts of a wagon road that dropped off down the hillside.

'Down there a piece. Matlow's found what he says is the best spot. It's just down the main trail a bit. It'll be quicker if we just take this short-cut.'

The drizzly rain that had been falling eased off, but Danny didn't notice. He was too busy trying to keep up with the older man and not slip or fall on the steep track. Finally, after what seemed like more than an hour, they came around a rocky outcropping and on to the wider, wagon-rutted main road.

Standing there with his hands on his hips, trying to catch his breath, Bartlett looked back up the hillside. In places he could see where the wagon road cut in wide sweeping zig-zags, snaking its way down on to the flats.

'Is this the trail that Old Allen and his oxen took?'

'Uh huh,' Hodges said, filling his pipe with coarse-cut tobacco. 'This is it. The main northern trail down into the river valley.' Pointing on down the road, he nodded, before using a wood kitchen match to light the pipe. 'It's about thirty miles or so down to Marysville and then a bit more to Sacramento. That's where the first gold was discovered, at Sutter's Mill. That wasn't so long ago, but most all the claims have been bought up by big mining companies. I hear there have been some discoveries being made farther north, up in the Oregon Territory, but I doubt there's much there.'

'Back east everybody's talking about how easy it is to get rich out here.'

Hodges chuckled. 'Yep, and there are a lot of pilgrims such as yourself who believe it. Truth to tell, the only ones getting rich are those who sell the picks and shovels to fools who want to dig up gravel in some cold-water creek bed.'

'So what about this stagecoach that's supposed to be carrying gold?'

'Oh, it'll be along. Our part of the plan is to settle down back in those rocks down there. That's exactly where the last wagon carrying gold was robbed. That's where Matlow said he'd meet us. We'll just wait for him. He'll be along, him and his bunch.'

'That skinny guy that was with him there in camp, you mean?'

'Yeah, that was Juan Valdez. He's a bad one too. You don't want him mad at you. Old Ned's got himself a couple others, too. "English" Bob Carr is one, then there's that Johnny Biles. I don't like any of them and wouldn't trust that whole lot very far. But it's damn hard to make beans nowadays and we gotta take work, paying work, when we can find it. One good thing is that it's also real hard to find good men, men you can trust to do their job. So I reckon there'll always be a place for us at the table, if'n we don't get too choosy.'

'I still don't understand exactly what this job is.'

'Just hang on there a little while; you'll have to learn as we go along.'

Hodges had time to smoke a couple more pipefuls before Matlow and three other men came riding down the wagon road. While waiting, he had suggested that they get back off the road a bit so not to frighten anybody riding past. Traffic on the road was light, only a couple of wagons and few riding horseback went by.

'Hey there, Ned,' Hodges called, stepping back on to the rutted roadbed. 'We about gave up on you.'

'Had to wait to make sure the coach was on its way. Here, kid,' he said, swinging out of the saddle and handing the reins over to Danny, 'make yourself useful. You take the horses off down the way a piece. There's a little draw down around that corner. Take them down off the road and keep them ready. Bring them out when I holler. Think you can handle that?'

'Yeah, I know about horses.'

'Hey, Ned,' Hodges cut in, 'I think he's going to do all right. Don't be so abrupt with him. All he needs is to be shown what he's to do.'

'Well, that's what I just did. Go on, take the horses down there and wait until I call then bring them back fast as you can.'

Danny nodded, took the reins of the four horses and headed down the road. Just beyond the corner he spotted the little ravine off to the right just as the big man had mentioned. Looking back he was surprised to see the

15

wagon road was empty. Hodges and the rest of them had ducked back into the rocks, he figured.

Pulling on the reins, he took the animals off the road and down the draw a dozen yards or so where he found a small grassy spot. A small seep of water pooled in a puddle before disappearing into the rocks. Letting the horses drink, he slipped the bits from their mouths to allow them to chomp at the grass.

Making himself as comfortable as he could on a big round boulder off to one side, he sat and waited. The late morning sun had broken through the rain clouds and it felt good. So good he had to fight to keep from dozing off.

This job still didn't make a lot of sense, but so far he felt he was ahead of things. He'd gotten a meal out of old Hodges, hadn't he? And even if he hadn't been told what he was getting paid, for sure it'd be more than he had in his pockets right now. The best thing he figured was to just wait and see. So far things hadn't worked out like he expected, but he could worry about that tomorrow.

Having made that decision, he sat back, letting the warmth of the sun begin to remove the dampness of his shirt. Looking the four horses over, he had to smile. They were a lot better horseflesh than anything that had ever been on the farm. Better than any horses he'd seen on the wagon train, too. Good, strong looking stock, the kind that would make travelling a pleasure.

Relaxed and feeling drowsy, he was brought to his feet and wide awake at the sound of gunfire back up the road. Gathering the reins, he was ready to move, waiting for that big man, Matlow, to call.

The rattle of gunfire died as quickly as it started and for a long few moments there was no other sound. Then, crashing out of the brush behind him, Hodges came running and sliding.

'Quick, get in the saddle and let's get the hell out of here,' he said, his words tripping over themselves. Grabbing one of the strips of leather, he swung up into the saddle and turned the horse down and away from the road.

'C'mon, boy. Move it. They'll be after us before you know it. Wake up and climb aboard or end up swinging from a tree limb.'

Not waiting any longer, Hodges spurred his horse out of sight.

Danny didn't understand, but the panic in the older man's voice made him move. Without thinking about it, he hoisted himself into one of the saddles and jammed his heels into the animal's flank. The surprised horse jumped and took off at a gallop the way the other had gone.

Ducking under the branch of a straggly tree limb, Danny heard the echo of Hodges' pards in his mind, something about swinging from a tree limb. What had he gotten himself into?

# CHAPTER 3

They rode hard for what Danny thought was miles. When Hodges finally pulled up to give the horses a breather, the young man almost fell out of the saddle. Riding down that draw, then up and over the top of a low ridge only to plunge down the other side, all he could do was hang on to the saddle horn, ducking under trees limbs and trying not to fall off.

'We got a little time,' Hodges said, climbing down and loosening the saddle cinches to ease the horse's breathing. 'I figure they'll be busy rounding up Matlow and the others. Unless one of the gang tells them, they won't know about us or the horses. That'll give us a chance to get away.'

Danny Bartlett, holding on to the saddle leathers, was fighting to fill his own lungs. Breathing easier and still holding on to the reins of his horse, he thought about what had happened.

'What was that all about? I heard some shooting and then you came crashing in yelling something about getting hung. What happened?'

'Boy, you really did just come off the farm, didn't you? I'll tell you what happened. That fool Matlow thought he was smarter than anyone. Well, I got to admit I never expected them to follow along behind. Not so close anyhow.'

'Who do you mean?'

'It was a bunch riding along to protect that gold shipment. They came around the bend and caught us flatfooted, yelling and shooting. I was standing near that string of boulders and ducked back in. Don't think anyone had a chance to see me. I looked out and saw that Juan fellow go down. Didn't see anything else, just took off. My luck I was just a little above where you had the horses.'

The youngster suddenly understood. 'Matlow and his

men were robbing that shipment, weren't they.' It wasn't a question. It was a discovery. 'We were helping him rob that stagecoach.'

'Well, I reckon. You and me were in the same boat. No money and getting hungrier by the minute. OK, I should have said something. I knew you didn't figure it out. But what the hell, I thought it was a quick way to get a stake. Enough so I could go on up north, maybe. There's talk of gold strikes farther up north. It was supposed to be easy, just stop the stage, take the strong box and ride out. You and me would've got enough to live on. For a while, at least.'

Danny shook his head. 'But now we're running from the law. And on stolen horses. Oh, gawd, what happens if we get caught?' He quickly remembered hearing the older man saying something about swinging from a tree limb. 'Oh.'

Hodges didn't say anything, just stood next to the horse watching his young partner's face.

'I can see I was wrong to get you involved, but, well, I knew we were both in the same fix. No money, no gold and no real way around that. I read somewhere that desperate men do desperate things. That's the way it is.'

Danny didn't have an answer for that. All he could do was stand there, holding on to the horse, and think about how things hadn't turned out as he'd expected. A few hours ago he thought he'd be picking up gold with both hands and now he was part of a gang of stagecoach robbers. The horse stamped a hoof, making him remember he was a horse thief, too.

Hodges quickly tightened the cinches and swung back into the saddle. Danny stood looking out over the tops of

19

the brush as if he was trying to see his future.

'We can't stay here any longer. Sooner or later someone will wonder about the horses that gang was going to use and come looking. Either that or someone will talk. They all knew my name and it's certain they'll not hesitate to talk about it. They don't know you, but for sure we were seen together in Gold Ridge so they'll have a description.'

'So what do we do, run? You think we can outrun them?'

'Uh huh. There isn't any real law in these mining camps. Gold Ridge is just like all the other camps. The law is made up of those men with something to lose. We get caught trying to rob a claim or one of the saloons, then a vote is taken and a hanging is held. You and me are far enough away from that fracas back on the wagon road; we keep riding and there won't be any one who cares. For damn sure we can't go back to Gold Ridge, though.'

'Can't someone question where we got these horses? They are both pretty fine animals, not the kind someone like me would be riding around on.'

'No. Nobody'll care about that. People don't ask a lot of questions. They're either too busy trying to make a living or they don't want anyone asking questions about them. But you're right, these aren't your usual long-travelling horses. Somewhere we'll have to find a swap, get us less delicate riding livestock.'

'We can't just go riding out. What about your tent? And your bedroll? It's all back in that camp of yours.'

'Yep, and it's probably already making someone else happy. We certainly can't go back. Far as my bedroll?

Well, whoever was riding these horses we've got was ready for travelling. In case you didn't notice, there are bedrolls and full saddle-bags tied on both these saddles.' Hodges stopped a minute and then chuckled. 'You know what? I'll bet that damn Matlow never expected to share any of that gold with you and me. I'd say his plan was to hit the stage then take off. Think about it. Those men had horses, we didn't. No sir, I'll bet we would have ended up standing there in the road waiting for that posse to come take us away. Damn the man's eyes.'

Somehow that didn't interest Danny Bartlett much. All he wanted to do was get away from the threat of a hanging.

# CHAPTER 4

It made Danny feel a little better when he discovered that nobody was paying them any notice. Of course for a couple of days they had been careful to stay out of sight, not riding any trails or wagon roads, keeping to the high country. There had been some food in the saddle-bags and even a little sack of coffee beans, but those supplies hadn't lasted long.

'We're going to have to find a town, you know,' said Hodges one evening as he fried up the last of the bacon. 'Don't know what we'll use for money, but this is the last of the food. Whoever packed these saddle-bags didn't figure on being gone long, or more likely they planned on heading over toward Sacramento. They could get lost in the crowds over in the bigger city.'

'What towns are up this way?'

'Well, I don't really know,' the older man said after a while. 'I reckon the first thing we'll have to do is head down out of these hills. It shouldn't be hard. Not everybody is gold crazy. There are people down in the flats that are making pretty good money growing what the miners are needing. I'd guess it won't be hard to find someone to point us in the right direction.'

'You think that's safe?'

'Yeah. We've come far enough away from Gold Ridge. There won't be anyone we're likely to run into that'll even have heard of that mining camp. But just to be safe,' he said, stroking his flowing beard, 'I think I'll cut this shrubbery back, maybe just leave the moustaches. Without it, I doubt even my own mother, God rest her soul, would know me.'

'There isn't anything I can change. Guess I'll just have to take my chances.'

Hodges chuckled, separating half the cooked fat back on to two tin plates. 'No, I don't think you'll have any problem. You haven't shaved in a while and the face hair you got will do. Makes you look just like any of a hundred or so young men coming out to find their fortune.'

They took their time eating the meagre supper, trying to make it seem like there was enough. Later, to further fool their stomachs, they lay back on their bedroll, and talked about where they came from.

Hodges started it off. 'You'd never figure me to be out here on a hillside counting stars if you'd seen me, oh, say

22

four or five years ago. I was a pretty successful business-
man back then. Owned a feed store in a little town in
North Carolina, it was. Knew everybody living within
twenty miles and was even thinking about standing for
mayor in the next election. Now, look at me, riding
someone else's horse and sleeping in his soogan.'

Danny, his hands clasped behind his head, thought
about his own background. A lot of times, growing up,
when the summer heat made his bedroom up in the attic
of the house too hot, he'd take his bedding and sleep
outside. Lying back watching the stars was a good way to
end the day back then. Now his life wasn't so peaceful.
Hearing the older man talk about the horses they were
riding made him break out in a sweat.

Wanting to think about something else, he asked
Hodges about his family.

'You have a family back then?'

Hodges was silent for a time. Danny could tell when he
finally answered that it wasn't a happy memory. 'Yeah, I
had a wonderful woman. Belle was her name. Yeah, a wife
and two little daughters, Elizabeth and Hester. It was a
good life, but then it all went bad. Belle took sick and
before I could get the doctor she was dead. Old Doc
Moser said it wouldn't have made any difference if he
hadn't been out to the Andrews' farm. Old lady Andrews
was having another baby and, well, even that didn't work
out. Both the mother and child died.'

Danny shook his head in sympathy. 'My ma died when
I was a youngster,' he said slowly, not wanting to think
about that either.

'I didn't handle Belle's death very well,' Hodges went
on, not hearing what Danny had said. 'I thought her

dying was somehow my fault. Oh, I knew it wasn't, not really, but the thought was always there. If only I'd done something different. There's no excuse for it, but I started to drink. Just to stop the remembering, you know? The drinking got real bad, so bad the business was going to hell. Hester, the oldest daughter, she tried to get me to stop but, well, all that did was turn her against me. Little Lizzie was too young, she didn't understand. Hester didn't understand either.'

Hodges wasn't talking to Danny any more; he was just talking, like he couldn't stop.

'I sold the feed store while I still had something to sell. Put the money in the bank for the girls and headed out. Ended up there where you found me, dead broke and not a nugget to show for my time in the gold fields.'

'You didn't go back? What about your girls?' asked Danny, and then stopping, knowing it wasn't any of his business.

'Huh? Oh,' Hodges said, sounding like he just come awake, 'no I never went back. You see, you're not the first young person's life I messed up.' After a little he rolled over to face away from the dying fire.

'It's time to get some sleep,' he said.

Danny lay there, watching the stars and thinking, until he also fell asleep.

# CHAPTER 5

Coming down on to the flat land of a broad valley the next morning, the two men found themselves riding on a well-used wagon road. Danny tried to relax but was worried about being out in the open and time after time turned to watch their back trail. Noticing a rider coming up behind them, he felt panicked and warned Hodges, then started to pull off heading into the brush growing alongside a little stream they'd been riding beside.

'No, don't do that,' the older man said. 'Just keep going the way we've been going. That jasper's seen us and if we were to duck off the trail he'd think we were up to no good. We keep riding and let him catch up; he'll be cautious but that's only natural.'

'How do you know he isn't someone who'll know about the stage hold-up?'

'Boy, you're going to have to stop worrying about that. You're letting it eat you up and that isn't doing any good. Just relax. That hold-up was news only to a few people in that mining camp. Nobody else will care. Now don't go to talking. Let me take care of it and maybe we can find out how far it is to some place.'

The rider came on warily, keeping his gun hand resting on his right thigh, close to his holstered sidearm. Hodges, using his right hand to touch the brim of his floppy hat, nodded and called out.

'Morning. I hope you can tell us how far we got to go to the next bit of civilization? We ate up the last of our grub this morning and need to see what we can do to stock up.'

The rider, keeping to one side of the pair, pulled back to match their slower pace.

'Well, the nearest town of any size is on up the valley, about ten miles or so. It's called Shasta City. There're reports of another gold strike up near there. You boys heading up to try your luck?'

Hodges chuckled and shook his head. 'No, sir. We've been seeing nothing but men up to their tender parts, standing in the cold water trying to squeeze gold out of the riverbed. Somehow I don't think many of them are doing so good. No, we figure there'll be some other way to make beans.'

Nothing more was said for a while. Still nervous, Danny caught the rider glancing at them from time to time. Slowly, hoping no one would notice, he moved his hand toward his right-hand pants pocket. He'd been carrying his pa's pistol there.

'Well,' the rider said finally, 'I can't promise anything you know, but you're only another mile or so to the turn-off to my pa's place. We're raising cattle and got another piece of land planted in corn. Now like I said, no promises, but I'm just coming back from Marysville. Pa had sent me in to see if I could hire a few men. I hate to have to tell him that there ain't none to be had. Everyone wants to get rich; nobody wants to work.'

Hodges glanced at Danny and nodded. 'Young Bartlett here was raised on a farm, but until I got the gold bug I ran a feed store. I'm afraid I don't know anything about cattle or corn raising.'

'You can sit a saddle, can't you? Most work we got going right now is to move some of our herd back down to Marysville. Pa's got a steamboat coming up the river in a couple weeks to take the herd down to San Francisco. There's a big market for fresh beef down there.'

When they reached the entrance to the ranch, without discussing it, Hodges and Danny followed along with the young rancher. The main ranch house was a couple miles off the main road. Seeing bunches of cattle here and there, Danny was impressed. They were all red and white Herefords and looked fat and market-ready.

When his son introduced the newcomers, Hank Rafters wasn't impressed. Young Henry, he thought, frowning, hadn't brought back the four or five hands he'd hoped for, but two seedy looking refugees from the gold country. They'd have to do. He'd agreed to have a couple hundred head ready to board the steamship Gov. Dana at Marysville in less than a month's time. Yeah, they'd have to do.

'I have to tell you right up front,' the elder Rafter said, looking the two men over, 'I don't think those horses of yours will be up to the job. Nice horseflesh, though. Yes, sirree. But they're just not heavy enough. All right, I'll hire you to help move a couple small herds down the valley to the loading docks at Marysville. Pay you each thirty dollars a month and found. There are three herds going, two about fifty head each and the last, a hundred head. Now, if that suits you, go drop your bedrolls in the bunkhouse over there,' he jammed a thumb over his shoulder, 'and come back up to the main house. Ma'll be putting supper on the table soon. After we eat, we'll see about getting you some working mounts.'

Danny wasn't all that happy about making trips to Marysville and he let Hodges know about it before going back up to the big house.

'I'm not sure we should be taking this on, Hodges. Isn't that where that big fella, Matlow, was going, Marysville?'

'No, that was the drover you rode into Gold Ridge with. I never did hear where Matlow was headed, but it could have been Marysville. More likely Sacramento. I figure him for the big city. That is if he got away from that posse up there. We don't know about that, now do we?'

'No, I guess not,' the youngster answered slowly, not sounding convinced.

'Boy, you're going to have to get over that. We're in luck, getting this work. Rafter said it's good for about a month. If we save our money, it'll be enough to get us to wherever we decide to go.'

'Yeah. Thirty dollars. I've never had that kind of money before. But what did he mean, and found?'

'That means he feeds us and gives us a place to bunk on top of our wages.'

Tossing his bedroll on one of the rope-sprung bunks, Daniel Bartlett smiled warily. The whole place looked a lot better than anything he'd had back at home.

Supper was thick slices of smoked ham, piles of mashed potatoes and a big bowl of dark meat gravy. Corn that had been canned and baking soda biscuits rounded out the meal. The two new hands were introduced to Mrs Rafter along with their daughter, Anna. After nodding, Danny didn't pay the women any attention, focusing more on his food. It was while passing the pitcher of cold buttermilk that the rancher brought up the topic of the horses Danny and Hodges were riding.

'Those look to me like blooded stock,' he said, not looking at either man but keeping his eyes on his plate. 'Fast, I'd say. You boys ever race them?'

Danny didn't look up or stop eating. He didn't know what he'd say if asked anything about the two animals. Hodges merely smiled.

'Oh, they can run, all right,' he said slowly. 'That's what they were bred for. But neither of us has raced them.'

The rancher nodded, then after a bit went on. 'We've got the summer fair coming in another couple months. Lots of horse racing goes on. If you're still in these parts, maybe you can make yourselves a few dollars. I don't think there's another horse around here that looks to be as fast as the two of yours. What do you reckon, Henry? Do you think old man Benberthy's quarter horse could outrun either of them?'

Henry Rafter didn't answer, just shook head.

'Course,' the elder Rafter went on, while spreading butter thick on a biscuit, 'you'd want to find someone smaller than either of you to ride them. It's Anna here that rides our horses. She's more comfortable on the back of a horse than walking.'

Nothing else was said about the horses until after the meal when Henry Rafter took them out to a large corral. Leaning against a railing and watching the half dozen horses mill around, the young man explained about his pa's comments.

'Old John Benberthy has the place farther up the valley. He and Pa have been friends since they came out here from Dodgeville. The only thing is, Benberthy has a brown quarter horse that's beat everything in the area and has for the last couple years. Boy, let me tell you, that upsets Pa some. I noticed how he looked your horses over and I knew what he was thinking. I'd say before you two ride out, he'll be making you an offer to trade. Now, let's get a rope on a couple of these and maybe get a couple hours of riding in this afternoon.'

# CHAPTER 6

The work of gathering the first small herd took three or four days. Rafter wanted to make sure the beef he was sending to the city's butcher shops were the biggest and best. Making sure to keep the youngest stock for breeding, the trail herd was finally segregated off in a fenced pasture.

'We'll start moving them in the morning, boys,' the rancher decided after making a final count. 'It's not that far down the road but I don't want to push them too fast. These beeves aren't due to reach the loading dock for another four days so we'll be able to take our time.'

The drive turned out to be hard on Danny's legs and thighs; he hadn't ever sat a saddle for so long at one time. Even though they were only moving at a slow, grazing walk, once the herd got moving Rafter didn't want to let the animals stop.

Danny Bartlett was learning a lot about cattle, both in the gather and during the long drive. The main thing he discovered was that cows were stubborn. It was all the four men could do, to keep them going in the right direction without wandering.

Old man Rafter took the lead each day and the others took turns riding drag. Danny was more than ready to be rid of the beasts by the time they reached the loading pens. After a lazy meal at one of the town's restaurants, the return trip only took one day's riding. Hank Rafter and his son stopped off at one of the larger saloons for a drink before leaving town, while Hodges and Danny turned down the invitation. Both wanted to get out of town as soon as possible.

Rounding up the second herd was done a little quicker than the first; both Danny and Hodges knew more about what they were doing. The only difference in the drive was that Hank Rafter decided not to go along. He told Henry to run things for him.

The drive went a lot easier the second time. As before, after leaving the fifty head at the loading pens, Henry paid for a dinner at the restaurant and invited the men over for a drink. Again Danny and Hodges said thanks, but would ride on out. They were sitting in the afternoon sun waiting when Henry caught up to them. It was obvious that he'd had more than one drink.

Cutting out a hundred head was even easier than before. Hank Rafter wasn't so choosy this time. Most all the breeding stock had been separated out and moved to another piece of range. The four men were able to make up the herd pretty much with what they found.

It took all four of them to make the last drive. After the

31

herd was tallied and in the pens waiting for the steam-boat, and the customary dinner eaten, Hodges and Danny rode back to the ranch alone. The Rafters had decided to stay over to meet up with the steamboat officials to talk about scheduling another shipment.

'You boys go on back out to the ranch,' Hank Rafter told them, 'me'n the boy'll be along tomorrow and pay you off then. Tom, you and Danny be thinking about a price for those horses you came riding in on. I'd surely like to own both of them.'

On the ride back, Danny and Tom rode side by side so they could discuss what they were going to do next.

'Boy,' Danny said, 'I've really enjoyed this and I don't mean just earning a lot of money, either. There was a lot of work back on Pa's farm but it wasn't anything like what we've been doing. That was the same thing every day where this, well, this was hard but a lot better than fol-lowing some plow horse down a furrow all day. You know what I mean?'

The older man chuckled, shaking his head. 'I have to admit, it was a lot more hard work than running a feed store. The most work I had to do back then was move around hundred-pound sacks of corn. But Rafter's let us know there isn't any more work here. I'm thinking we ought to go on, head north maybe. Hell's fire, maybe we can find some more work on another ranch.'

'Well, I don't know about going back to hunting gold, that's for sure.'

Hodges chuckled. 'As I recall, you came over the mountains and before even picking up a shovel, got involved with that plan of Matlow's. I sure do feel bad about that, but that's water over the dam. And I do agree, hunting gold's not a good way to spend our time.'

Thinking their own thoughts, they rode a while in silence.

'You know,' Hodges said after a bit, 'I have to agree with you. These past few weeks have been pretty nice. Oh, it wasn't fun, the first few days. I thought my butt would never get used to sitting a saddle all day, but I sure feel good today. And with some pay coming, too. Look out there,' he said, waving a hand in the direction they were riding, 'that's good river bottom land. I'd say a man could grow anything in that soil.'

It was Danny's turn to laugh. 'Well, I for one don't want any more farming. No, sir. If I can, I'd like to go on doing my work on the back of a horse.'

'I saw a place somewhat like this once,' Hodges said, thinking back. 'It was when I was coming out west, travelling with a wagon train. We'd got to an army fort, Fort Hall it was, and the people I was with voted to take a new trail down along the Humboldt River. You got to remember; I was just sobering up in those days and wasn't really paying too much attention to very many things.' He paused, remembering. 'To be honest, I didn't really care much about anything at that time. Anyhow, the vote was taken and the wagon I was riding in took off north, up on what was called the Oregon Trail. Someone going on over the mountains into the gold country asked if I wanted to ride along with them. I didn't much care, but went along. One thing I do remember was coming along a nice little valley at one point, one that looks a lot like this one, only not so wide. Don't know exactly where it was, though. Somewhere a little north of a dinky little town named Union, as I recall.'

'Yeah,' said Danny, remembering, 'that's about the same way I took getting to California. Fort Hall was where the wagon trail split up for the bunch I was with too. You know, that would be mighty good, to find a place something like this.' Recalling the stagecoach hold-up and not liking it, Danny quickly went on, 'like this, only a long way from the California gold country.'

The rest of the ride went steady. They weren't in a hurry, just enjoying the day. Neither man offered any suggestions about what they would do after leaving the Rafter ranch.

Mrs Rafter served up her usual meal, lots of meat, potatoes and biscuits, topped off with apple pie. It was Hodges and Daniel's practice after supper to carry their evening cup of coffee and walk down past the barn and lean against a corral railing and talk about things. They'd barely got comfortable when they heard a horse coming at a gallop up from the wagon road.

Henry Rafter, his hat flying over his shoulder, hanging on by the chin strap, came racing into the yard. Jumping out of the saddle before his sweat-lathered horse had come to a stop, he ran toward the house. Danny and Hodges hurried over to see what was going on.

Seeing the two men coming across the yard, young Rafter called out. 'Boys, there's been trouble. You better get your gear together. I gotta talk to Ma, then I'll be out.'

'What's the trouble?' Hodges called. 'Where's your Pa?'

Henry stopped at the top of the porch and looked back. 'We was robbed as we came out of town. Pa went back to get the sheriff. He thinks you may have something to do with it. Now, don't go wasting any time. He's bringing the law.'

# CHAPTER 7

That's all it took to get Danny moving. Before young Rafter reached the house, he was headed at a run for the bunkhouse. Hodges stood by the corral for a moment, thinking, then climbed through the railings and, taking a lasso, roped two of the horses there. It was a matter of minutes to toss their saddles on the horses and cinch them down. Danny had taken about that long to roll up the bedrolls and put the rest of their gear in saddle-bags. Hodges was just finishing getting the horses ready when his young partner came back. Henry Rafter was coming at a run from the house.

'Yeah, that's good thinking,' Henry said, his words coming fast, 'getting those horses saddled. No, look, here's the best I can do,' he said, handing a packet of money out to Hodges. 'Listen, instead of thirty dollars, I've doubled that. If you'll take the money and those two horses, I'll tell Pa that that was the trade we made for those two racers you rode in on.'

Hodges took the money and, opening the gate, led the two horses out.

'Tell me something,' he said, tying his bedroll on the back of the saddle, 'You say your pa was robbed of the money he got for the herd? How'd it happen that he's blaming us?'

'Oh, hell,' said Henry Rafter, looking past the two men toward the road, 'the first thing he said was that someone had to have told the robbers that we'd be carrying money. He thinks one of you must have told someone we'd be delivering a bigger herd.'

Hodges frowned. 'But you know neither of us hung around town after running the herd into those loading pens. Every time Danny and I rode out of town, we waited until you or you and your pa finished your business.'

Young Rafter frowned, but didn't look at Hodges, keeping his gaze on the road toward Marysville. 'OK, so maybe that last time, when I went in for a drink, maybe I talked too much. But don't you see,' he suddenly turned to look pleadingly at the older man, 'I can't let Pa know that. That's why I'm making this sweet deal for you. Look, you're leaving anyhow, ain't you?'

Hodges wasn't through yet. 'And what made him jump to the conclusion that it was us who talked out of turn?' he asked, looking steadily at the younger man.

'Don't you see? It's those horses you rode in on. They're what made him think you fellas were riding one step ahead of the law, you know? Two out of work men riding fine animals like that? Have to be highwaymen of some kind. That's his thinking.'

Hodges didn't speak, just stood there waiting.

'OK,' Henry said when he saw nobody was moving, 'Look, I'll throw in a packhorse and load it up with enough supplies to get you down the road a good piece. Now that is all I can do – the supplies, those two horses and a hundred dollars each. That's in trade for the horses you rode in on. Now don't be hesitating too long. I tell you, Pa is bringing the law out from Marysville.'

Hodges slowly nodded. 'A hundred dollars each, huh?' He glanced at Danny who was sitting his saddle. 'All right. We'll take the blame for your mistake. Like you say, we're leaving anyhow. You better get busy putting together those supplies. I'll get the packhorse ready.'

Danny took a long look down the wagon road when they rode out, but didn't see anybody coming. Even if Rafter and the sheriff were pushing their mounts, it'd still take them well after dark to get to the ranch. Dropping in behind Hodges and with the rope to the packhorse, he gigged his horse.

They rode out of sight of the ranch before Hodges reined away from the road and headed back up into the foothills. The country they were riding turned dryer once they left the well-watered bottom land. Bunch grass and low-lying Manzanita brush covered the slopes. It had been about an hour or so before dark when they left the Rafter's place but there was still enough light to see where they were going. Finally the older man pulled up next to a small fast-running creek. The place he'd chosen was a small grassy meadow in the middle of a small stand of pine trees.

'This is far enough for tonight,' he said, swinging down out of the saddle. 'No call for us to be hurrying now. We still got enough light to see just what kind of supplies young Rafter paid us off with. I'll break things out while you start a little fire. We can have another cup of coffee before turning in. I figure this is a good time for us to talk about things a bit.'

Danny didn't say anything, but did as his partner said.

After putting hobbles on the horses he dropped the bedrolls next to the saddles and quickly gathered up enough sticks and dry tree limbs for a fire.

Hodges had laid everything out on his blankets and was looking it all over when Danny came to see. 'Well, the youngster did his job right, I'd say. He even stuck a rusty gold pan in one of the panniers and tied a short-handled shovel to the pack frame. Now if that isn't to make it easier for us to make our way farther up in the gold fields, I don't know what is.'

The crushed coffee beans had boiled by the time he got everything put back in the hard leather panniers.

'I have to admit, he gave us a good start. I'd say we're a lot better off than we were before we rode in to that bit of work. By the way, here's your share of our payday,' he handed the small cotton sack of coins over to Danny. 'With what we got in those leather bags and the money, we can go a long way.'

'Yeah, but I don't like riding away like that.'

'What do you mean? He paid us off a lot more than what we earned.'

'That's just it, more'n half that money he gave us was for those horses that didn't belong to us to sell. And now, on top of being wanted for taking part in that stagecoach hold-up and riding out on someone else's horses, the law back in Marysville will be after us for something we didn't have any part of. It just seems to pile on, you know what I mean?'

Hodges, sitting on his bedroll with his back to a fallen tree trunk chuckled. 'Oh, I doubt the law in Marysville ever heard of us, or for that matter about any cattle rancher being robbed either. No sir, the way I see it, the

Rafters, father and son, think they pulled a big windy on us.'

'What do you mean?'

'Think about it. Hank Rafter wanted our horses. OK, so they weren't really ours, but he didn't know that. He thought we were probably some kind of outlaws riding away from some crooked deal. The only type of cowboy that'd be riding such fine animals would be outlaws or big time cattleman or the like. So here we come. He takes one look and decides to bamboozle us. Now he knows those horses are worth a lot. Certainly a lot more than what he ended up paying for them, a couple hundred dollars and a pair of work horses. Throwing in a pack-horse loaded down with enough to get us a long way out of this country, well, that didn't cost him too much, I reckon. To make it work, and to get us on the road out as fast as possible, he has his boy come busting ass in, yelling there's been a hold-up and you two are being blamed. Uh huh, and we, already one step ahead of the law, are quite willing to play our part and head for tall timber, thinking the law is one step behind. Yes sir, I'd say that was the game they were playing.'

'You don't think Mr Rafter got robbed?'

'No, I don't. If all what young Rafter said, his pa was bringing the sheriff and all, why did he come ahead to warn us? Because we couldn't have been the ones warning our outlaw friends about the bigger herd coming in and the blame would fall on him? Say the law did come out and we sat there saying it wasn't us who talked about the pay-off for that herd. Who would anyone believe, the son of the robbery victim or two questionable characters who happened to be fitting the description of outlaws anyhow?'

'Then that's more reason to go back. To clear our name of something that might not have happened.'

Hodges chuckled and put a match to his pipe. 'Clear what name? Ours? Who's going to bother about that? We'd get laughed at if we went in and told some story about a wealthy rancher not getting robbed and blaming us. No sir, I'd say we came out of it pretty good. The only question is, what do we do next? Do you want to ride on up north? Remember there was a discovery talked about happening somewhere up there.'

Danny's coffee had grown cold but he sipped at it anyway.

'No. From what I've seen, digging for gold isn't going to get me what I want.'

'Now, what exactly is it you think you want?'

Danny was quiet for a time, thinking about it. 'I grew up on a farm and I've had all that I can handle. You know, working down there for Rafter was about the best work I've done. Maybe that's what I'll do; go try to find another ranch that's looking for men.'

Hodges sat, puffing at his pipe, thinking. Finally with a nod he glanced over at the younger man.

'You know,' he said slowly, 'I've been thinking. There's that stretch of valley I recall seeing back over the mountains. Now that was pretty good country and I doubt if anyone's put a claim on it. We could. Set out the stakes and register it. The money we got wouldn't buy us much in the way of breeding stock, but I'll wager that when Rafter came out to California he had much more. Now I'd say that there's something to think about.'

Danny sat quiet, staring into the dying campfire. Then

jumping up, cursed.

'Damn it all to hell!' he exclaimed. 'I'm not going to do it. Not like this.'

The older man sat quietly smiling. 'I wondered what you were thinking about. Tell me what you're not going to do.'

'Simply ride away, letting those two run our name into the mud. I know what you're going to say,' he went on, holding up a hand. 'They don't know our names. But I'm tired of running from something I had no hand in. No sir, this isn't over. Not yet.'

Hodges knocked the dottle from his pipe. 'And what exactly do you plan to do about it?'

Danny stood quiet for a minute looking into the fire but not seeing it.

'I don't know. But something.'

'OK. I'm with you. Let's sleep on it and see what we can come up with.'

# CHAPTER 8

Lying back, looking up at the star-filled sky, Danny let his mind wander. Memories of when he was on the farm, bone-tired after a day of following a plow, but unable to sleep. Thoughts and dreams of a different life keeping his mind churning. Slowly his eyes grew heavy and, as back then, the darkness of sleep seeped in like fog along the river bottom. Letting himself float his body relaxed.

No! Wide awake he sat up. No, gol' darn it all, it just wasn't fair.

'Hodges, are you asleep?'

'Well,' the older man said sleepily, 'if I was, I'm not now. What's troubling you?'

'It just isn't fair. Look,' said the younger man, throwing off his blanket and standing up, 'we go riding off into the night while that cattleman and his son laugh. Why? Just so they can come out winners at the races at the next summer fair. While we ride away with them laughing at us. No, sir. It just won't do.'

Sitting up, Hodges poked at the coals cooling under the coffee pot. 'So, what do you have in mind?'

Danny stood staring into the darkness. 'I think we ought to take that away from them. Yes, I think that'd only be the right thing.' Looking at the older man he smiled, 'do you think we could get back to the ranch before daylight?'

'Well, yeah. But what then?'

Danny chuckled. 'C'mon, let's see what things are like back there.'

Kicking dirt over the bed of coals, the pair saddled up and rode back down out of the pine forest and back on to the valley floor. Holding to a walk, they quietly rode along, stopping only when they could make out the big barn buildings in the weak moonlight.

'Now what?' asked Hodges.

'Let's leave the horses here and get a little closer.'

No lights showed anywhere as the two skirted around the long bunkhouse and, keeping to the shadows as much as possible, came up to the plank side of the barn.

Listening to the silence, Danny tried to think of what to do next. A horse's hoof thudding somewhere inside the barn was all it took.

'C'mon,' he whispered.

Feeling along the side, he stopped before stepping out of the shadow. Moonlight made the ranch yard a grey expanse. Quietly and not hurrying, Danny eased along until he came to a small door. Slipping the latch, he quickly stepped inside. Hodges was right behind him.

Remembering the layout of the barn, Danny walked down one aisle to the line of stalls. The thoroughbreds that had once been theirs were in the last two.

Slowly, letting the horses smell them, each took the halter of one and quietly backed them out. Instead of going back to the front, Danny opened the rear door just wide enough to let the animals walk through.

Keeping at a walk, and again trying to stay in the darkest stretches of the night, they circled around the bigger corrals. Not hurrying, they soon found themselves back where their saddled horses were hidden.

'Damn it, boy, I think we did it,' said Hodges, laughter in his words. 'Now what are you planning on doing with these animals?'

'Well, how about we move them on down the road a piece, say somewhat closer to that other ranch, huh, Benberthy's? Our friendly cattleman will have a hard time proving these horses came from his place, won't he?'

'Yeah, and that'll serve him right. C'mon. Let's get this over with so we can still get a little sleep.'

# CHAPTER 9

The next morning, after a quick breakfast and using what was left in the bottom of the coffee pot to put out the camp fire, without talking about it they headed farther up into the mountains. It was during a brief stop to give the horses a breather that the question of where they were going came up.

'I figure from where we are to where that little valley was is on the other side of this range,' said Hodges, filling his pipe and using a kitchen match to light it. 'We've been climbing all morning so I got to think these would be the Sierra Nevada Mountains. From what I can recall we'd have to go on over these, then maybe another smaller range. I can't remember exactly. . . oh, yes, I do, someone said they were the Trinity Mountains. Anyhow I'd say, without looking at a map, that we're less than a hundred miles. Now, we got enough grub that if we get some deer meat, even if we don't come upon a ranch or store, we can make it that far without starving.'

He waited a little to give his partner time to think about it before going on.

'If we didn't lollygag around we should be able to make it that far before very long. Least ways we'd get across these mountains and that'd be good.'

'Well,' Danny said finally, 'this California country hasn't done much good for me. I'm all for taking a look over that way.'

Riding up into the high country, slowly making their way over the Sierra Nevada, gave both men a lot of time to think. For young Bartlett it was the feeling he was running away that filled his thoughts. For the first couple of days, he continued to watch their back trail. Whenever they topped out on a ridge, he'd stop and for long moments sit looking over the forests they just ridden through.

Mentally shaking his head in disgust with it all, he was just starting to rein his horse around to go catch up with Hodges when he saw movement below.

The place he'd been watching was a line of scrubby pines at the edge of an acre-sized clearing. He remembered coming into that little opening, giving the horses a moment to drink from a small stream.

'Time to take a break?' Danny had asked, 'give them a breather and a bit of grass?'

Looking up at the sun, Hodges nodded. 'But not here. I'd feel better if we were on higher ground. Maybe stop and make up a bit of lunch. A cup of coffee'd be just about right, don't you think?'

Now sitting still, he watched as a man on a dusty brown horse stopped, letting his mount drink. Whoever it was, he was wearing a big, floppy-brimmed hat. Unable to see the stranger's face didn't bother Danny. He wouldn't know the man anyway.

Moving slowly, Danny reined his horse around and eased on into the trees behind. Hodges had gone on, stopping to wait for the youngster a short distance ahead.

'There's a rider coming behind us,' said Danny. 'Think it could be someone from Rafter's ranch?'

'What'd he look like?'

'Couldn't tell. He's on a big brown horse and wearing a wide-brimmed hat. That's about all I could see. He stopped about where we did to water the horses.'

Hodges shook his head. 'I don't see any reason for anyone from the ranch to be chasing after us. Hell's fire, that was days ago. They'd more likely be busy squabbling over the ownership of those thoroughbreds than following us. No. More'n likely it's just someone doing what we're doing, riding up into the high country. Let's ride on a bit and see if he follows.'

They'd been following a game trail, signs of deer droppings showing the trail to be well-used. Riding higher through the forest, Hodges slowly changed direction, leaving the trail, riding through the widely-spaced trees. Topping out over a narrow ridge, he rode on until he found a place that satisfied him.

'This'll do. We'll tie our horses down there,' he said, pointing down below at a small stand of high brush, 'and wait and watch.'

The spot he'd chosen gave them a view down the slope they'd just ridden up. Anyone coming would be out in the open a little below them.

'Danny, see that tree there?' Hodges pointed to a single tree twenty or thirty feet to the side. 'You sit yourself there and wait. If this fellow comes up, he'll see me sitting here. That'll give us a chance to see what it's all about. Don't do anything, let me see what's what. Oh, and take your pistol. Just in case, you know?'

Settling in with his back against the lone tree, Danny tried to be calm. Hodges didn't seem worried but he was. Slowly, as nothing happened, he started to relax. From where he was sitting he had a good view of down the

46

slope they'd come up. He wasn't sure exactly where they'd ridden, the sunshine openings made shadows in the trees darker. Birds flittering in the tops of the forest below caught his eye. He smiled, thinking how peaceful everything was. The smile faded when the rider came through the trees.

Slowly, his head turned side to side as he came at a walk into the open. With his gaze sweeping his surroundings, he stopped when he spotted Hodges. Instantly sliding out of the saddle and staying on the downside of his horse, the man stood motionless.

From where Danny sat, the man was on the far side of his horse. All the youngster could see was the floppy-brimmed hat. Danny didn't move.

'Well, look who we have here,' called out the stranger. Danny thought he almost sounded as if he was laughing. 'I expected you to hold up sooner or later. *Sí, amigo.* All I had to do was follow along and I'd find you. Now, where is the young one?'

'Juan Valdez,' said Hodges, slowly getting to his feet. Calmly dusting the dirt off his butt, he watched the man standing a short distance below him. 'Now why are you following us? Last I saw of you and the others, a bunch of angry men were shooting at you.'

Danny heard the man chuckle. '*Sí*, ah, they were very angry. But not very good shots. No. Like you, when they came at us, I slipped into the rocks. Whew, it was for a little bit a small war, you know?'

Danny recognized the man. He'd been the one with Matlow, the one Hodges said was a bad one. Then he'd been wearing fancy leather pants with shiny bangles down the legs. Under the horse's belly Danny could see

47

there were no bangles on the man's pant legs now. The pants looked like the same canvas kind most men wore. He wondered if Juan Valdez was still carrying a pair of pistols as he'd had on back then.

'So,' said Hodges, sounding calm, almost friendly, 'you got away. And now you're here. Wonder how you did that? And why?'

# CHAPTER 10

'Ah, *señor*, you were easy to follow. When I got far enough away, well, I looked for the horses you were supposed to be holding. Sadly they were not there. So I, um, borrowed another and rode away.' Danny frowned when the man chuckled. '*Sí*, and decided to continue riding away. That was supposed to be an easy thing, Señor Ned had planned for. But it turned out not to be. So I rode on. Thought I would try further north. Men digging gold are usually stupid men. Can you believe my surprise to find those horses we had stolen to use in the stage hold-up in the corral of some rancher? Ah, old man, I was so angry. I had great love for one of them but now the rancher had my horse and I could not prove it was to be mine. So I came looking for you.'

'You came looking for me because someone had your horse? Your get-away horse? That doesn't make sense.'

'Ah, but *sí, señor*, it does. To me it makes good sense.

48

You see, I think maybe you got away with some of the gold those men were carrying. Or maybe you met with Matlow and would know where he is. I find him, maybe with gold from that wagon. Then I would get what I had been promised. You see, *amigo*, it makes very good sense.'

Hodges slowly filled his pipe and, keeping an eye on the other man, touched the tobacco with a match. 'You're following us thinking we got away with some of the gold. Then the others, Matlow and Biles, didn't get killed?'

'No. Some did. Bob Carr was wounded. I think they hung him later. I do not know for certain. And maybe Ned or Johnny Biles got a little shot up, I don't know. But it remains, you may have some of the gold. So I follow you. I have nothing else to do, do I?'

Danny watched as the two men stood facing each other, here in the forest miles from anywhere, talking as if on a street corner. Hodges looked relaxed, his pipe in one hand, the other hanging at his side, and the Mexican smiling and chuckling.

While they were talking, Juan Valdez had moved to his horse's head and was gently scratching at the animal's nose. 'Where is the boy you are riding with? I do not see him.'

'Well, he's around. But to get back to it, I didn't come away with any gold, and I certainly don't know where Matlow or any of the others are. Fact is, I don't believe there was ever going to be any gold come my way.'

Valdez laughed. 'Ah, you are a smart man. No, Señor Ned was not good at sharing gold with anyone. So you do not have the gold and don't know where Ned Matlow is? Then, why are we talking?'

Danny watched as Valdez, with his body turned a little, hiding that side from Hodges, pulled his pistol holding it at his side. Thinking to warn his friend, Danny stood up and hollered.

'Watch out, Tom!'

Surprised, Valdez turned to look, then seeing his mistake turned back and raising his pistol, pointed it at Hodges. Not hesitating, Hodges had raised the Walker Colt he'd held at his side and shot the Mexican. Twice.

# CHAPTER 11

'Damn!' exclaimed Danny, seeing a cloud of smoke blanket most of the shooter's upper body. He hadn't seen Hodges' gun before and didn't know the older man was carrying it. 'That surely caught him by surprise. Me too.'

Hodges smiled as he went about reloading the two cylinders. 'It's a Walker .44 caliber. Uses black powder, that's why there's so much smoke.'

Once the gunsmoke cleared, and Valdez's horse had settled down, the two looked at the dead man.

'Thanks for the warning, Danny. I figured him for something like that but your calling out threw him off.'

'He really did think we had some of the gold, did he? I can't believe he'd think that.'

'Well, he didn't know how things had turned out. I guess chasing after us or riding north, he made the wrong choice.'

'So what do we do with him now?'

Hodges smiled, and went on reloading his Walker. 'Nothing. I reckon we'll take his belt and guns and leave the rest. That's about what he'd have done, had he shot you and me.'

'Just leave him? Shouldn't we bury him or something?'

'No reason to. Pretty rocky here, be hard to dig. Anyway, even if we did put him in the ground, animals would have him dug up before sunrise tomorrow. No, we'll leave him. Take his horse, though. No reason to leave the poor animal to fend for himself, is there?'

Danny didn't like the idea of stripping the man's gunbelt off his body. Rather than argue with Hodges though, he simply wrapped the weapons up with the belt and shoved it all in one of his saddle-bags. He didn't like leaving the dead man lying there either. It didn't seem right, somehow. To make it all worse, they now had an extra horse they'd killed a man to get. Was everything always going to be like that? The best thing, he decided, was to keep riding, heading east, away from this country and all the get-rich-quick people here.

Hodges knew what was bothering the younger man and decided it was up to him to do something about it. Anything to keep the youngster's mind off things. Slowly he started teaching his partner. One of the first things was how to live off the land.

Things started in that direction early one morning, shortly after the run-in with the Mexican gunman, when they were breaking camp. While loading up the pack-horse, Hodges looked up in time to see a small herd of deer slip out of the trees across the small creek flowing through the meadow they'd stopped near. Catching Danny's attention, he motioned him to silence. Slowly taking his worn looking revolver from a saddle-bag, and never making any sudden moves, he stepped over a few feet to lean against a small pine tree. Using the tree to steady the weapon, he geared back the hammer and aimed at the nearest deer. Holding the gun steady, he eased back the trigger.

The blast sounded like thunder, breaking the morning silence. In a flash the half dozen or so animals broke for the trees, disappearing instantly. Only one, after taking a short leap, didn't make it.

Danny had heard the loud explosion of the handgun back when Hodges had shot Valdez, but then it'd happened so fast it hadn't registered.

'Lordy, that sounded like a cannon,' said the youngster. 'It's a wonder more than one of that herd didn't fall down.'

'Yeah, the piece of lead from this old handgun dropped that doe pretty quick didn't it? Come on, we got some work to do.'

The rest of the morning was spent butchering the animal. After hanging the carcass from a tree limb and pulling the skin free, Hodges went on to cutting the deer meat into strips. It took some time, and while he was at it he had Danny build a set of racks using long thin willow branches. That was the beginning of teaching the younger man what he needed to know.

'We might as well set up a more permanent camp,' said Hodges, 'while we let this venison dry in the sun. It'll take a couple days but it'll give us enough meat to last quite a while.'

While watching over the drying meat strips, Hodges dug the wide, shallow gold pan out of one of the panniers.

'You never got around to using one of these, did you?'

'No.'

'Well, I doubt there's any colour in this little creek and if there is it'll be farther up, not down here in this bit of flat land. But using it correctly should be part of your education.'

Hodges explained that gold, being a lot heavier, would lie in the gravels along the creek bed up closer to where the creek flowed off the hillside.

'Takes a good flowing stream to move the bits of colour along. That's what happens, gold-bearing material breaks off because of weathering or gets broken up during winter run-offs. Takes a long time for the bits and pieces to get moved downstream. All that time, while the gold is being rolled and rubbed against rocks and gravel, it gets broken up even more. Nuggets get smoothed out and what gets worn off is mostly what shows up in the bottom of a gold pan. There's a knack to using one, though. I'll show you how it's done.'

A few days later they packed up and moved on. They hadn't found any gold but they had a sack made out of the deer hide filled with sun-dried meat. After that when coming to any fast-moving stream that Hodges thought just might be likely, one or the other would use the shovel to dig down to bedrock and pan what gravels they found. Once or twice little specs of the yellow metal were found in the bottom of the pan. It wasn't until they were on the far side of the Sierra Nevada that the empty tobacco sack they used to store their findings started getting heavier.

They were close to running out of supplies when, after shooting a second deer and taking time to dry it in the sun, they found the Spanish gold mine.

# CHAPTER 12

The first batch of sun-dried venison was about gone and at the same time they had run out of coffee. Their small load of supplies had lasted until they were somewhere down in the lowlands after leaving the Sierra Nevada mountains. The next mountain range was still a dark purple haze on the horizon. Hodges thought that range was probably the Trinities. They'd made it that far when they brewed up the last of the coffee beans.

'Damn, I'm not going to like starting out the day without coffee,' Hodges said, sitting back in the failing light, taking his time to savour the last of it. The coffee had been carefully stretched out, using and reusing the crushed beans until there was nothing but pale brown water being poured before mashing more beans.

'About all we've got is what's left of the deer meat. I've been keeping watch, halfway hoping we'd come across some sign, but it's like nobody's ever been here before.'

As before, Danny had been watching their back trail too. 'That valley you were telling me about, was there anyone close to that?'

Hodges sat thinking about it. The time he'd come any-where near this way was with the wagon train he'd joined. He'd been helping drive along the train's small herd of cattle when they came down the trail from Fort Hall. He tried to remember what he'd seen.

'There was a little bit of a town somewhere along there, while we were following the Humboldt River. It wasn't much more than a saloon and store, all one build-ing. I can picture it but I'm not sure exactly where it was in relation to that valley.'

'So, we're out of coffee and soon out of everything else. We can't exist long on nothing.'

'Well, Danny, since we left the mountains I've been watching for anything looking like food. Haven't seen a thing. You got to keep in mind I don't have many loads left for the Walker. I didn't look but that pair of pistols the Mexican was packing probably came fully loaded. How much powder and shot have you got for that pistol you said you were carrying? You know, I've never seen that gun. What is it, anyway?'

Danny went to his saddle-bags and dug around until he came up with a cloth bundle. Unwrapping the slightly oily piece of cotton he smiled, thinking about his pa handing it up to him as he sat on old Bess.

'Here, son,' his pa had said. 'You're sure to need some protection. Just be careful with it. No gun is dangerous by itself, but if it isn't used right, it's the most risky thing there is.'

Holding the gun he paused, thinking about his pa, wondering if he was still working his farm. This time of year he'd be harvesting the last cutting of hay, ricking it up for the winter. Finally he handed the heavy pistol to Hodges.

'Oh, Lordy,' Hodges said, hefting the weapon in one hand. 'I haven't seen one of these in a long time. You ever fire this?'

Danny shook his head. 'No. Pa had an old muzzle-loader we used for hunting. I didn't even know he had this until I was leaving the farm. That's when he gave it to me.'

'An Allen & Thurber pepperbox revolver,' said Hodges almost reverently. 'Back home, along with the feed store, I dealt a lot with firearms. It started when someone wanted to trade his rifle for a sack of seed. Times were tough there for a few years and, well, when business picked up again, I found I had acquired quite a few rifles and pistols. Pepperboxes like this one were pretty popular. See, it's got six barrels that revolve when the hammer is dropped firing the gun, instead of a cylinder revolving like with the Walker. It don't look like it's been fired much, and,' he went on, snapping the barrels open to check the loads, 'I'll bet the moon that the powder you've got in here is useless.'

Using the rod that he pulled from the circle of barrels, he shoved the bullet and gunpowder from each barrel. The powder dropped out into the palm of his hand in a little pellet.

'Yeah, see? Sometime or another your powder got damp and clumped up. Well, I expect we can dry it out and it should work. Nothing wrong with the bullets.' Holding the barrels so he could peer down each one, he snorted. 'These don't look too good. Been too long without oil and they're a bit pitted. I don't know that I'd want to hold on too tightly if it did fire. Probably take your hand off, too.'

Danny didn't like the sound of that. 'It was Pa's gun. I guess I'll hang on to it.'

'Well, we get to someplace civilized, we'll have to stock up on powder. Was there any powder or lead in that wrapping?'

Laying the oily cloth out, Dan picked up a small waxy sack, which he handed to the old man.

'Ah, good, if we can dry out what was in the barrels and with this we got enough powder. Now all we need is for something to shoot at.

As if someone had been listening, the next morning, coming up over a little rise they looked down on a small flock of antelope drinking at a seep.

# CHAPTER 13

Antelope meat wasn't as tasty as the venison, but neither man complained. With a handful of wild onions they found growing in a swampy area thrown into the pot, the thick stew Hodges cooked up was filling.

The weather was changing by the time they left the tree-shrouded slopes of the Sierra Nevada mountains. Out on the flat lands, they soon found themselves riding across the beginnings of a desert. Instead of trees, there was clump grass and some kind of heavily-scented brush.

Juniper, Hodges said. It took nearly four days of riding to cross the dry plains. Reaching the slopes heading up into high country, Danny saw that even the juniper had thinned out.

Since killing the antelope, the odd jack rabbit was the only animal they saw. Not wanting to waste any gunpowder on them, Hodges simply set traps each night. Most mornings saw them holding two or three of the little carcasses, about enough meat to get through the day. The horses seemed satisfied with the sun-dried grasses they found.

The Trinity Mountains weren't as high as the Sierra Nevada and topping out over a high ridge, Dan glanced back. He was surprised to see the highest of the mountain range behind them was covered with snow.

'Hey, Hodges, look there. We got across just in time. It's winter back there.'

'Uh huh. I figure we're on the down slope of these mountains now. Not likely we'll run into much snow from here on. Not enough to bother with, anyway. But if we don't find food and water in the next day or two we'll wish we had some of that white stuff.'

The water they found was a series of springs about halfway down a steep-sided narrow canyon. Water flowing from a dozen or more seeps and springs came together to form a creek that gushed and gurgled across the bottom of the deep ravine.

'I think we'll have better luck down there,' said Hodges, sitting his saddle and taking his time to give it all a close look. 'We'll take it easy going down. I wouldn't be surprised to find deer sign down close to the water.'

The deer he shot an hour or so later was bigger than

the others had been, and it took the best part of the day to cut the meat and hang it out. With the sun only hitting the bottom of the canyon for a few hours in the middle of the day it took longer to dry the meat too. The camp they set up was made more permanent with the addition of piles of boughs they cut from a small grove of pine trees they found a mile or so upstream.

Where they set up camp was on a wide section of the ravine. A small meadow on a bend of the creek gave them grass for the horses and a halfway soft place to bed down. It was Dan who spotted something that didn't belong. He had been half dozing, his eyes moving lazily along the far canyon wall, going from one long streak of white rock to another. Letting his gaze drift he noticed something unnatural; a wide round stone standing on its edge next to a series of ball-shaped piles of gravel. The stone looked to him like a wheel.

'Hey, Hodges, what do you make of that? Somehow it doesn't look like anything nature would do. Looks somewhat like a stone wagon wheel. Least ways there's only the one.'

The older man had been working on a piece of deer hide, making another bag for the dried venison. Looking up to see what Danny was talking about, he frowned. Setting aside the deer hide, he got up and walked over to inspect it close up.

'That, son, looks like what's left of an arrastra.'

'What's that?'

'It's a crude machine used to bust up the quartz to get the raw gold out. That's what those white streaks are all along that wall are, quartz. You see, this here stone, when it was working, there'd be a wood axle through the

59

middle of it. That's what the miners would hook their mules up to. When the mules walked around in a circle the big wheel-like rock would turn, crushing the mineral rock placed on the flatter base. You can bet that thing has been there a long time, too.'

'You mean someone's been here and dug up gold?' Danny said, glancing back toward where the creek pooled up.

'Wouldn't be surprised. But not like over in California, not with the gravel in that creek bed. Not if they were using that arrastra. Nope, and it wouldn't have been done any time recently, either. See that tree growing out of the pile of gravel over there? That gravel pile is rock crushed to get the gold out. It's been there long enough for the tree to grow. A long time.'

'You know, now that you mention it, it looks somewhat like the old grist mill my pa used to take some of our wheat to. The miller would make flour using a couple of big stone grinding wheels.'

'Same idea, only instead of grinding up wheat, the miners here were grinding up rock.'

'Who would have been around back then, to be working a gold mine? I never heard of any Indians that were interested in getting rich.'

'Nope. It wouldn't be any Indian. Most likely Spanish explorers, I reckon.'

Later, after a meal of venison cooked by hanging the meat on sticks near the fire, the two set back to enjoy the evening. Settling back by the dying campfire, the older man filled his pipe and, using a coal from the fire, set the coarse shreds of tobacco burning. Danny had just started to doze off when Hodges started talking. The old man's stories were always filled with things the younger man had never heard of before.

'That little valley we're heading for, I figure it's only another couple days on the other side of these mountains. I figure that little town I was telling you about is likely a bit farther on. Probably something like another week or so riding. Long time to go without anything but deer meat to eat, but there it is.'

Danny, sitting and staring in the fire's coals, didn't say anything. Thinking about some of the meals that rancher's wife had cooked up made his mouth water. To stop thinking about ham and mashed potatoes, he decided to think about something else. Gold.

'So you figure this was what some Spaniards found?' he asked quietly, waving a hand back over toward the pile of tailings.

'Well, yes, I'd say so. I read about it in a book once and figure that arrastra was the kind of equipment they'd have used.'

The two men sat for a time staring into what was left of their camp fire, not talking. Once again it was Danny who broke the silence.

'You think they got all the gold there was to get?'

'I reckon it's certain they got all the gold that was easy to get. I doubt if they left much behind.'

'I wonder,' said Danny, then stopped thinking about it. Glancing over at his partner, he shared what he'd been thinking about. 'You know, even if we find that valley you talk about, we're still going to need some cash money to buy enough stock to get started. How are you planning on us doing all that?'

This wasn't the first time Danny had thought about

this but he'd always been afraid to bring it up until now. What would he do if the old man was thinking about holding up another stagecoach or even a bank to get enough money to buy a small herd? That was the answer he didn't want to hear.

'Well,' said Hodges after a bit, 'I've given that some thought myself and have to admit to not having come up with any answer yet. Now you ask about the Spaniards getting all the gold. Maybe you're on to something there. Maybe we should take a closer look at these old workings. You never know, do you?'

Ignoring the lack of coffee or something to eat other than dried venison, for the first time in a long time Danny felt good. Maybe things were going to turn out all right after all.

# CHAPTER 14

The next morning, after a breakfast of venison steaks washed down with cold water, Danny took the shovel and gold pan and started working the gravel in the creek bottom. Stopping in the heat of the day, when the sun was overhead, he had turned up nothing.

Disgusted he sat back on his bedroll.

'Unless I'm not doing it right, I'd have to say there's no gold in that creek. Looks like those Spaniards had the right idea and dug their gold out of the canyon wall.

Wonder how they knew where to look?'

Hodges had spent most of the morning building racks out of thin willow branches he cut from the brush crowding the creek banks. He had kept an eye on the younger man and now smiled.

'Oh, I think you were doing the panning like I showed you. As far as the Spaniards, well, I'd say they had lots of experience, searching as they did all over the place for gold. They'd see something like those streaks of whiteish rock over there. Quartz rock, it is. I recall hearing how veins of gold can sometimes be found in that kind of rock. Could be 'cause gold melts quicker and when nature heats things up it just naturally pours into breaks in the harder quartz. Yeah, I've been told that's a good indicator. But this creek isn't much for length and isn't likely to hold much in gold. What they call placer gold is the kind that comes out of rivers and creeks. Hard rock gold taken from a mine would be different, rough and usually in smaller pieces. Not likely to find much of that in your pan.'

'So we'll have to find another way to stock that valley we're heading for, if we ever find it. How long do you think before we can move on out of these mountains?'

Looking up at the sky, Hodges shook his head. 'I don't think we'd better stay around much longer than we have to. Winter'll be coming on any time and if we sit around we'll end up spending the winter without more supplies than we got. We can't live on antelope or deer meat very long. I reckon we'll be ready to head out of here in a couple more days.'

The two men spent most of the rest of the afternoon sitting with their backs against a big boulder, each thinking his own thoughts. Tom Hodges' mind was on gold. He'd been thinking about the work the Spanish explorers had done. It was hard to picture how they'd done it. Probably coming north out of Mexico looking for places like this little canyon. Those white streaks of quartz would likely catch their attention. Breaking any gold-bearing quartz down had to be hard work. Lying there thinking, it came to him to wonder where they would have found enough gold-bearing quartz to make it worthwhile.

Thinking about it, but not wanting to get his young partner excited, he didn't say anything. Nodding to himself, he got up and stretched.

'This sitting around is making me lazy. Think I'll take a walk around, see what there is to be seen. Want to go exploring with me?'

Danny thought about it a minute then shook his head. 'Guess not. Sitting here in the quiet with the sun warming things up is too nice. Beats sitting in a saddle for hours on end. You go ahead. Yell if you find anything interesting.'

The problem with just sitting, though, was while the body wasn't moving his mind was. Seemed like any time Danny wasn't busy his mind went back to worrying about getting caught and hung for his part in the stage robbery. As bright as the sun-filled canyon was, the young man was no longer sure that things weren't getting darker all the time.

It didn't take long for Hodges to find where the miners had been digging. All along the far wall of the canyon were piles of the rough white rock. At a couple places they had dug holes. He found only one that could actually be called a mine. He couldn't see how far the hole went back into the rock wall. Lighting one of his kitchen matches, he hunkered down and peered into the darkness. Before the fire got too close to his fingers, he thought he'd seen enough. Calling it a mine was questionable, as the hole only went back ten feet or so.

'But,' he explained later when telling Danny what he'd found, 'the rock making up all these piles of tailings had to come from somewhere. So likely they did find gold in that bit of a mine shaft. Probably dug until the seam of gold ran out and quit digging.'

Danny, looking the rock piles over, nodded. 'These Spanish explorers, they had to have travelled over a lot of country before getting here. You know, they must have found a lot of gold in their travels.'

Sitting back, relaxed with his back against the boulder, Hodges nodded. 'Had to, to make it worthwhile. Look at the grinding stone they used to crush the quartz. It took a lot of work just to chip that wheel round enough for it to do its job. Now they weren't likely to go to that extreme unless they had found a profitable looking outcropping.'

'How would those men separate the gold from the rock once it was crushed?' Danny asked, trying to picture it.

'Well, I don't know. I suppose they might have used a pan in that creek there, working the broken up rock like you were doing with that gravel. Or maybe they simply stopped the wheel from turning and picked out the gold from the bits and pieces of loose quartz.'

'What then? Do you think they'd brush the broken-up bits and pieces of rock out of the way for the next batch to be crushed?' Danny was almost able to visualize it when the thought struck him. 'You think it might have happened that way?'

Hodges didn't answer, just shrugged his shoulders.

'Then,' Danny went on, getting into his new idea, 'isn't it possible they didn't get all the gold? I mean if they picked up what they could see, couldn't there have been smaller bits and pieces that went into the tailings with the broken up quartz?'

Neither man said anything for a while, thinking about it.

'Well,' said Hodges finally, 'I'd say there's one way to find out.'

Getting the shovel and the pan he moved over to the nearest pile and started digging. Taking a pan full of the finest of the crushed-up rock from the very bottom, he began swirling it in the creek water.

'Well, I'll be damned,' he said after a few minutes. 'Danny, we may have found how we're going to buy our herd.'

In the bottom of the pan, mixed with fine white sand were a few threads of yellow. For a long moment they could only stare at what they'd found. It was Hodges who broke out laughing first. Danny's smile grew until he couldn't hold it and then he joined in. A coyote that had been skulking closer to the source of the drying meat he had smelled jumped at the sound of the loud laughter that suddenly filled the canyon, made louder by the echoes.

# CHAPTER 15

The two men worked the closest pile of tailings left so long ago by unknown Spanish explorers. Danny did most of the digging with Tom panning the gravels in the creek. This work went on for the next four or five days and slowly the old tobacco sack filled out with the jagged bits and pieces of gold. It was a sudden drop in temperature one night that caused them to think about how late in the season it was getting to be.

Loading up the packhorse, the pair left the narrow canyon and made their way down and on to the plains. Once again, they stretched the last of the sun-dried meat as far as it'd go. Tired and hungry they stumbled into the town of Union a day after the last of their food ran out.

Danny Bartlett had been hungry before but he didn't think he'd ever been as hungry as he was the morning they rode into town. All thought of food went when the first person he saw on the churned up muddy main street was wearing a badge. Instead of food, the fear he'd been living with came back churning his stomach.

'Tom,' he said, reining back and turning half around, 'what'll we do? There's a lawman coming down on us.'

Hodges had seen the man too, but hadn't noticed the badge. He had thought to ask the man where the town's bank was.

'Settle down, Danny, my boy. Just settle down. You're

not thinking. There's no way in hell this fella would know about what went on clear over in the gold country. Don't go getting all panicky now.' Lifting a hand, he called out to man wearing the badge. 'Hey there, could you give us some information?'

Standing with his hands on his hips the sheriff nodded. 'Sure can. By the looks of things I'd say you were a couple more refugees from over the mountains.'

Danny held his horse back a bit, watching as Hodges swung tiredly to the ground.

'Refugees? I don't know about that,' he said, pulling off his weather-beaten hat and brushing ineffectually at it. The dirt had coated the matted felt so long it had become part of it. 'I just know we've got a little business with the banker before hitting the nearest restaurant for everything they got on the stove. And I think these horses deserve a little attention, too. We'll have some business to talk over with whoever runs the stable.'

The sheriff, a stocky overweight man, his belly hanging over the buckle of his gunbelt, chuckled. 'Well, gents, there's a stable back behind the general store. And the nearest thing we got to a bank is at the general store. Now it so happens that right next door to that is the Union Saloon. Henry, the bartender, not only pours his own beer and whiskey, he also serves up a good meal, cooked by his wife, Sue-Ann.'

'Well, that makes it easy,' smiled Hodges. 'Having the stable right behind the store and the saloon and restaurant next door. I'd say someone has a corner on the town's businesses. Say, what'd you mean, refugees?'

The lawman chuckled. 'Oh, we get 'em all the time. Men coming back after finding out there ain't that much easy pickin's over in California and are heading back to home. I gotta say, you two've got the looks of it all right. Fact is it appears you might have stayed a mite longer than you should have. I mean no offense. It's just that you both look like you've reached the end of your tether.'

It was Hodges turn to chuckle. 'Yeah, no offense taken. I suppose we do look pretty bad, but we aren't heading back to home. No, sir. We stopped a few places on the way over the mountains and, well, we can pay for our supplies. Once we meet with the banker, that is.'

'Hmm,' drawled the sheriff, holding up a hand, 'if you two've got money or a little gold, I wouldn't be letting too many people know. Times are pretty hard for most of the men here in town. Seems most of them tried it over there and stopped here hoping to find some way to get on east. I'd just be a bit cautious is what I'm saying.'

'We will be, and we thank you for the warning. Now, Danny boy,' Hodges turned to look up at his partner, 'let's be taking care of the business of seeing about filling that stomach of yours. Thanks again for your help, Sheriff.'

'You're welcome and my name's Ben Catlin. They gave me the badge a while back 'cause nobody else would take it. You look me up, there's anything else you need. And welcome to Union, Washoe Territory.'

Hodges didn't climb back into the saddle but walked his horse on toward where the sheriff had pointed.

'Washoe Territory,' he said, glancing up at where Dan sat his horse. 'I never heard it called that before. I thought we'd be in Nevada Territory. Anyway, you feeling any better now? That lawman didn't pay any attention to us other than as a welcoming committee of one. You have to relax. Acting like that, you're making yourself look to be guilty of something. I tell you, nobody's going to know about that screwed-up robbery. No. If anyone's going to wonder about us, it'll be because of our having that extra horse. All saddled up and all. I figure one of the first things is to see if we can sell it.'

Danny sat his saddle, shoulders hunched over obviously feeling bad. Stomach knotted up with worry, but still growling.

Looking up at his young partner, he frowned. 'Now don't go getting all concerned. We aren't robbing the dead. Probably, if it's as hard here as that sheriff said, nobody'll give us too much for it anyway, saddle and all.'

Hodges nodded, trying to think of how to ease Danny into relaxing. 'C'mon, Danny. Think about it,' he went on keeping his voice calm and reassuring. 'What happened back in Gold Ridge was long enough ago even those folk there would've forgotten, or moved on. Now, we're going to see about turning some of that Spanish gold into cash money and then get food. So climb down and try to act natural.'

Still feeling uncomfortable, the younger man nodded and swung down to walk alongside his partner. 'I reckon you're right, but I've been worried about it for so long, it got me getting all sweaty when I saw that star on his vest.'

'Stop thinking about it and you'll be OK. Now, let's see what we can do in here.'

Tying the horses to a railing, the two pushed through the door and into the store. Being hit with the odours of the stock made both men's stomach growl. It'd been a long time since Danny had been in a store like this one and he stopped to simply stand there looking first this way and then that.

'Gentlemen,' the man standing behind a plank counter called, 'and how can I help you today? New to town, aren't you?' he went on, stepping closer and looking them over. Stopping a few feet away, he frowned. 'Now I gotta be clear. I can't sell you anything unless you can pay for it. This isn't a charity store.'

'Now that's all right with us,' declared Hodges, smiling and making his words soft and friendly. 'We're here to deal with the bank. According to the sheriff we're in the right place. Does that make you the banker?'

That made an instant change in the man's attitude.

'Well,' he said, smiling and dry washing his hands. 'Yes, I maintain some banking services back here. My name's Watkins, Cecil Watkins. If you'd come back here, we can see what's what.' He pointed toward the rear of the store and moving back, waved them to follow. 'It started when someone wanted to sell this old safe. He'd planned on carrying it over into the gold fields, thought he could make a business, start up a bank over there. Damn fool got it this far and nearly killed the horses pulling his wagon. I made him a good offer and opened up my own bank.'

'Can you handle gold dust?'

'Oh, most certainly. Most of the banking business I get is with gold. Folks coming in from California, some of them got a little dust and are buying supplies to carry them on back east. Is that your plan, gentlemen?'

Danny almost laughed. His idea of what a gentleman would look like didn't match how he knew they appeared. He let Hodges go on doing the talking.

71

Tom Hodges must have had the same thought. 'No,' he said. 'What we want is to turn enough of this,' he dropped the tobacco sack on the counter, 'so we can buy dinner and get a change of clothes. These we're wearing have just about seen the last of being wearable. We'll be loading up some supplies before leaving town, though.'

Watkins opened the bag and poured a bit of the gold into a pan hanging from a small scale.

'Well,' he said, looking closely at the yellow metal, 'I hardly think this came from California. This isn't placer gold at all. No sir, I'd say someone dug this out of a quartz outcrop. Uh huh. Hard rock gold. I don't get to see much of that.' Looking up, he waited to see if either of the two men were going to say anything. Neither did.

'Well, yes. Now the going price for gold is twenty dollar the ounce, you know. The government back in Washington DC sets that price. Well, to be honest, it's a few cents over twenty dollars, but I only pay out twenty.'

As he talked, he poured more of the gold into the pan, adding tiny weights on to the other side until everything was in balance.

'All right now, there's exactly two ounces. Do you want me to weigh out the rest of it?'

Hodges glanced at Danny before shaking his head. 'No, I figure it'll be a lot easier to carry around if we keep it in that tobacco sack. Just take enough to pay for what we'll be needing.'

'All right then,' said Watkins, 'let's stop there. That should be enough and if need be we can weigh out some more. Now,' he went on, dropping his voice and becoming serious, 'I don't know where this came from and I don't guess you'll be telling me. However, if I were you, I certainly wouldn't be letting anyone know it wasn't placer gold you brought in. That's what people will expect you were carrying. It's what all the others have. There are those who find out it was hard rock gold and that'll get them curious. That might not be the safest thing to do. You understand, the people living around here are good folks, but times are hard and money is scarce. Just a word of warning.'

'For which we thank you, Mr Watkins. Now, Danny, let's pick us out some new pants. And those boots you're wearing are getting mighty thin, too.'

# CHAPTER 16

Once they had finished the heavily loaded plates of steak and potatoes put before them in the restaurant, both men sat back, relaxing with a second cup of coffee. When they had sat down for their meal, the pair had taken a table at the back of the room and Danny put his back to the door.

'Man,' said Hodges, leaning back in his chair and filling the bowl of his pipe, 'there's something about a meal that's been cooked by someone else that makes it so much better, even when it's only pan-fried steak and boiled potatoes.'

'I'm looking at a piece of that apple pie.'

The older man chuckled and put a match to the tobacco.

'Well, we found this town just in time. That's the last of my tobacco. What do you say we load up the packhorse and head out of town? I figure we can be a few miles closer to where we want to be by nightfall.'

Danny frowned and then nodded. 'That's fine with me. We can't get away from town too soon to satisfy me. Tell you what, I'll stay back there in the stable and rub down our horses while you make up the supplies. I'll meet you out front.'

'Danny, you're going to have to get over this. You're letting what happened over the mountains become too important.'

'That's not so easy. It doesn't seem to bother you at all, but just being around people, I can't relax.'

'OK, I give up. Go on and finish your pie and go tend to the horses. I'll meet you out front.'

When they had walked around to the stable thinking to sell the extra horse, they had talked it over and Danny had agreed to let the older man do the bargaining. At first the stableman hadn't been too interested in buying Valdez's horse. Even with the heavy big-horned saddle.

'They's too many coming in to sell and not enough wanting to buy,' he complained, all the time running his hands over the animal's legs and inspecting its hoofs. 'Now this is a pretty good horse. Been taken care of some. That saddle, it's good for a lot of years left in it, too. But, well, I don't know.'

Hodges and Danny stood silently, waiting.

'Tell you what,' said the stableman finally, 'I'll give you fifty dollars. That's the best I can do.'

Hodges pursed his lips and frowned. 'Well, I can see what you mean. Times here are tough. But, well, it wouldn't be right, letting old Charlie's horse go so cheap. Charlie was a good man to ride the river with. He hadn't got snake bit, he'd be here today. No sir, I reckon we couldn't let old Charlie's horse go for less than,' he hesitated, 'seventy-five dollars.'

Finally they agreed on sixty dollars and the stableman would throw in feed and stalls for the other three horses while they were in town.

Now with a full stomach and feeling drowsy, Danny was brushing down their horses. Working away back in the coolness of the stable, he noticed how all three had started putting on their winter coats; the hair on their flanks was longer. He wondered if that meant the coming winter would be harsher. The grooming took a little longer than he thought it would, but as he saddled the two and settled the panniers on the packhorse, he got the feeling all three animals felt better for the brushing.

His pa had been a stickler for making sure the draught horses used to work the fields were brushed at the end of each day. Thinking back on those times, Danny almost wished he'd never heard of the California gold fields. Leading the animals out of the stable and into the alley-way next to the general store, he shook his head. No, even with all the grief and trouble he'd run into, this was somehow a better life than back on the farm.

That thought made him smile. His thinking disappeared when he heard Hodges yell out. Looking up, he saw his partner at the mouth of the alley fighting off two men. Without thinking about it Dan reached into his saddle-bag grabbing his pepperbox pistol. Not taking the time to aim, he pointed the barrels at one of the men and touched the trigger. Through the cloud of black smoke, he saw the man clutch at his chest and fall. The other attacker, bending over the body of Hodges, looked up then turned and ran. Dan didn't have a chance to fire again.

# CHAPTER 17

Dropping the reins, he ran to where Hodges lay and knelt beside the old man's body.

'Tom, are you all right?'

'Oh, gawd,' the older man moaned, holding his head with one hand. 'What'd he hit me with?'

Drawn by the gunfire men came running. The first to reach them was Sheriff Catlin.

'What the hell's going on?' he called, coming around the corner of the building. Seeing one body lying in the dirt, he stopped, then came closer. 'A hold-up? Someone musta found out you were packing that gold. Damn. Is your partner hurt bad?'

Dan shook his head and helped Hodges gain his feet. 'Tom, are you going to be all right? Should we find a doctor?'

'No, I'll be fine,' Hodges muttered, still holding his head. 'I swung around just as he hit me and lost my balance. I was falling when that one bashed me with a gunbutt or whatever he was using. It only clipped my head. I'll be OK in a minute.'

'There were two of them, Sheriff,' said Dan. 'The

other one ran. I couldn't get a shot at him.'

'Too bad.' Turning the dead man's head so he could see the face, Catlin nodded. 'Yeah, I've seen this one around. Anybody know who he is?' he asked the half dozen men who were crowding the alley.

Watkins the store owner answered first. 'No, but I think he was in the store about the same time these two and I were doing some banking business. I saw him going through a pile of shirts, but didn't pay him any mind.'

Someone else said he'd seen this one and another man over in the saloon. 'I don't think they been in town long. I only saw them that one time.'

'Well, it's likely his partner won't stick around now,' the sheriff said. 'Boys, I sure hope this doesn't make you feel you're not safe in Union. We haven't had anything like this happen in a long time. At least a week or two.'

'Well,' said Tom Hodges, tenderly touching the small knot on his scalp, 'I guess we were some lucky, Sheriff. Least I was. Darn lucky Danny here was quick enough to get a shot. Probably saved me from really getting hurt.' Turning to his partner he smiled warily, 'but I think we'd better do something about that pistol of his. A six-shot pepperbox does the job, if the barrels turn and you can get more'n one shot off. Let's go see what's available in the store.'

Later, having left town, they stopped in a little grassy open place in the scrub brush a few miles out to make camp. After hobbling the horses and spreading out their bedrolls they boiled up a pot of coffee and settled back to talk over the day.

'I never did really thank you,' Hodges said, once he got his pipe burning the way he liked it, 'for stopping those bastards from working me over.'

Danny was silent for a time, deep in thought. 'You know, I've been thinking about that. That was the first man I've ever killed.'

'Now, Danny, you don't want to let that bother you none,' said Hodges quickly. He was afraid the younger man would go feeling bad about it. 'You did what had to be done. That's all. And you did it naturally, protecting our gold.'

Danny shook his head. 'I didn't give the gold any thought. Seeing him hit you I didn't even think, just dug out Pa's old pistol and shot him. No,' he paused and then slowly went on, 'somehow I don't feel bad about it. I should, killing someone should bother me a lot, but it doesn't. Back on the farm I hunted and shot my share of deer but it should be different, shooting a man.'

'Maybe you feel that way because you were protecting me.'

'What's strange,' Dan went on as if not hearing what Hodges had said, 'is that I stood there talking to that lawman and never once thought about him, you know, worrying that he'd ask about that stagecoach robbery. It's like you've been saying, it don't bother me. I didn't even think about it. I wonder how that happened.'

'Well, I don't know as how I could say. Maybe it's just part of your growing up.'

'Maybe.'

Hodges thought it was time to change the subject. 'What's strange to me is your being adamant about reaching for that old pepperbox pistol of your pa's and not one of the pistols we took off that Mexican back-shooter.'

Danny grimaced. 'You know, it didn't even cross my mind. Pa's pistol was all I was thinking about. Anyway, I

78

didn't want anything more to do with that man's guns. Damn glad that storekeeper was willing to buy them. Maybe I'm being silly, but I feel better about that now.'

# CHAPTER 18

Hodges laughed. 'Well, for sure the gun we bought you won't ever let you down. I'd heard about the new Colt Dragoon. It's a lot like my Walker except the Walker is pretty well known for the cylinder blowing up. You know, the US Calvary carries the Dragoon? They got used to them in the war with Mexico. You hear about that war?'

'Uh, I read some about it. The US fought off the Mexican army and ended up owning most of what had been the Texas Republic. Pa was always interested in all that, more than I was.'

'Well, if we're to take up ranching around here some-where, it will end up mattering.'

'How? What can the war with Mexico over Texas have to do with us?'

'Simple. The US government wants to own what's known as the California Territory. By going to war with Mexico over Texas, President Tyler figures he'll end up with California. Probably make it a state. I don't believe he cares about Texas, just wanted to get Mexico on the run. That's why he sent his representative out to California. A man named Fremont was out in San

Francisco some time back. I read about it. You know, I think he and his party came along this same trail I did. Anyhow, he and his men got California to form a republic and claim independence from Mexico. Now that gold's been found it only makes it more likely that California will become a state. Think about it, if California, just over that mountain range there, becomes a state, do you think this area won't be part of it? Yes, sir, I'd say if we go into ranching now, it won't be long before this territory becomes a state.'

Dan had had enough of what might happen or not. 'Thinking about ranching, where do we go from here?'

'Well, the Humboldt River is back that way, other side of Union. So let's keep heading a little north, keeping the Trinity Mountains on our left. The valley I saw back then has to be pretty close.'

The valley they finally decided on was a good four-day ride out of Union and, looking it over, both agreed it was near perfect. Running mostly north and south, it was protected from any northern blasts of weather at the upper end by a jagged range of mountains. Another lower ridge angling off to the south gave them a boundary in that direction. A small river flowing south from the foothills turned more southeast about halfway across the valley. Not a big river, the banks appeared to be stable. It looked like it could provide water year around. They set up a permanent camp nearby, just a bit off the valley floor, choosing a spot close to the top of a small hill.

A storm raged overhead the first couple days and they spent the time sheltered under the makeshift canvas tent they had bought in Union. Unable to keep a fire going they huddled in their blankets, eating cold rations. When the sun finally came out, they got busy digging into the side of the hill.

While Hodges dug, Dan cut a pile of small pine trees from a stand a mile or so up in the foot hills. Using these logs, they constructed a three-walled shelter, the fourth wall being the back of the hole into the hillside Tom had dug. Roofed by a foot-deep layer of sod, their new home was snug and dry. Hodges built a deep fireplace centered in the dirt wall with rocks brought up from the river. With that they were ready for winter.

With little to do, the partners spent the winter months making their soddy as comfortable as possible. Bringing more pine logs and saplings down from the high country they constructed a few pieces of furniture and a good-sized lean-to barn and corrals for the animals.

Being house-bound didn't sit well with the younger man. Even back on Pa's farm there was always work to do. Since leaving, he'd been going somewhere, heading for something. Sitting around listening to the wind howl wasn't that something. Maybe, he started thinking, trying to make a ranch wasn't either.

# CHAPTER 19

One morning when the sun was warm, the sky a brilliant blue, Hodges declared spring had arrived. Dan looked at the snow still covering the mountain tops to the north and shook his head. Almost overnight the grass down on the flats had begun to green up. Finally, after a couple days of being warm while sitting outside enjoying the sunshine, Dan had to agree. Maybe, he decided, his partner was right. This was a good place.

It was even better when they rode out and started driving stakes, formally laying out and marking the ranch boundaries. It took more than a week of riding and when they finished Hodges figured they had about a thousand acres of good grassland staked out.

'We'll have to make a trip back into Union soon,' he said one evening after the supper dishes had been washed up. 'Seems like we're always running out of coffee and tobacco.'

Dan nodded. 'Yeah, I've been thinking that, too. How does this sound, you've talked about writing a letter to your daughters and we're going to have to register our claim. So, you have more need to ride in than I do. What say you ride in, take care of business, get supplies while I ride back over to see if I can find that Spanish mine.'

'Gold bug still got you?' Hodges chuckled.

'Not so you'd notice. But if we're going to stock this grass we're calling a ranch, we're going to need money. I figure I can dig out enough to get a good start on it while you're in town.'

Through the winter, they had killed and hung the meat of one deer on racks along the back wall. Another carcass had been hung outside and allowed to freeze. Even with the slim rations they had, Dan had been able to put on a little weight and now stood just under six feet. Keeping the firewood split and piled high had given his shoulders and upper body a chance to toughen up.

Hodges, on the other hand, didn't appear to have changed, except for letting his beard grow out.

Finally agreeing with Dan's plan, Tom Hodges rode out on the same morning that the younger man headed up into the mountains.

Remembering the way they had gone when leaving the narrow canyon, or ravine as Hodges called it, he rode north a little, looking for a way up over the nearest ridge. When the two men had ridden out of the canyon with the Spanish mine they had taken time to study the surrounding mountains.

'This is something to think about,' Hodges had said, reining his horse around at one point. 'Things look different from different angles.' He sat, taking a moment to pack and light his pipe.

They had just come out of the canyon and into a wider valley. This one was as dry and rocky but wider. It ran in a more north south direction.

'Now,' he said once he got his tobacco burning right, 'if we wanted to come back one day, what would we look for to be able to find this place? I reckon that ravine there is just like any other. Coming as we did from the other end, if we were to try to find it from this end we'd never do it. They all look about the same, don't they.' It wasn't a question so Dan didn't try to answer.

'Even when you're just out riding around,' said the older man, 'it's a good idea every so often to take a minute to see what your back trail looks like. I notice you haven't been paying so much attention to that since we got into the Trinity's, not like you did after leaving Rafter's place, but you should. For different reasons. Now, what kind of landmarks do you see if you someday wanted get to this place again?'

Dan let his gaze travel around, looking first close by and then farther out. 'Well, there's not much that sets that canyon or ravine off. Except for those two thin peaks back there. They're the tallest and the sharpest in that range of mountains. They look sharp, like a pair of knitting needles. The mouth of the ravine is just about exactly in between them. I don't know what else there is. That old pine tree growing all alone over against that big rock does a good job of marking the place, I guess.'

'Well, yes, if you're coming back before it dies or gets knocked down. But those two peaks, now, they're the thing to remember. From where we're sitting, you're right, the mouth of the ravine is in between. Line up that tree and you'd be just right. All right, enough lesson. Let's ride on in a southerly direction and see where this little valley leads. I figure the valley we're wanting is more to the east of here, probably over that next low range. Keep watching and remembering, that's the ticket. A good habit to get into.'

Remembering those twin peaks and how they looked, Dan rode on, keeping his eyes open. He rode for four days before coming to the conclusion he was lost.

'Horse,' he said, sitting slack in the saddle, having stopped on the highest ridge he could find and looking out in all directions, 'the sun's going down over yonder so that's west. But I'll be damned if it all don't appear to me to be the same everywhere I look. What do you think? See anything familiar?'

The horse didn't answer, just went on chomping at a clump of bunch grass growing thinly between the rocks.

Nudging his mount with a heel, he rode down off the

ridge looking for a place to make a small fire and lay out his bedroll. Maybe things would look better in the morning.

He went to sleep wondering how old Tom was getting along.

# CHAPTER 20

Tom Hodges was tiredly slumped in the saddle as he rode into Union. The long trip over the mountains, even taking it as easy as he had, had left him feeling worn out. All during the long nights in the cabin waiting out the winter storms, he had found himself thinking about his family. This was something he hadn't let himself do since leaving them behind, not wanting to feel the guilt. Now, however, he was too tired to fight it.

As weary as he was, he couldn't help smiling to himself as he thought of Belle. They had met soon after he had opened his feed store there in Zebulon, North Carolina. From the very beginning the store did well and the morning when Isaac Collins came in turned out to be extra special; he was accompanied by his daughter, seventeen-year-old Anna Belle. They were married a year later.

Their first-born, Hester, was born squalling. From the very first, even before the midwife had left to help with another birth, the tiny baby, all pink and wrinkled, was telling the world she was here. Somehow the little girl child was able to yell out her screeching cry without seemingly stopping to take a breath.

Hester was celebrating her sixth birthday when Belle informed her husband that she was with child again. Elizabeth was the opposite of her sister. Where Hester was loud and demanding, Lizzie, as she was called, simply smiled and gurgled. Growing up, this difference remained. Both Tom and Belle felt their lives were complete.

'I worry, though,' Belle said whenever one of her friends commented on her family, 'my mother always warned that nothing lasts forever and getting too full of yourself is the beginning of the end.'

As if it was foretold, the good life didn't last. Tom had come home one evening all fired up; he'd been approached by a group of the town's leaders with the idea of putting his name up for the mayor's position. Belle smiled at the news, but wasn't as excited as her husband. Saying she was a little tired, she went to bed right after supper. The girls, Hester, feeling she was an old maid at twenty, and Lizzie, fourteen, cleaned up the dishes and completed their other duties. Tom sat with his pipe, deep in thought, planning for tomorrow and all future tomorrows.

Belle didn't get out of bed the next morning and seemed more listless and even more exhausted. Hester was sent to fetch the doctor that evening.

'Tom,' said Doctor Moser, accepting a cup of whiskey-laced coffee after examining Belle, 'I don't know what's wrong. She doesn't have any aches or pains, just is lethargic. I gave her a cup of herbal tea that will purge her system. Possibly that inner cleansing will rid her body of whatever is causing her sluggishness.'

The purging herbs didn't make anything better and the woman simply got weaker and weaker. Four days later Belle died.

For a time after the funeral, the three family members worked hard at getting their lives back in some sort of order. Hester stepped into the role of lady of the house as if she'd been born for it. Lizzie was young enough she bounced back quite readily, while Tom started spending more and more evenings at the Cattlemen's Club.

The Zebulon Cattlemen's Club had been formed in the recent past as a place the businessmen of the community could socialize. Until then the movers and shakers had made use of one of the town's many saloons. The liquor sold in both kinds of establishments was about the same.

Tom had never been a drinker, but he was finding it impossible to get to sleep without blotting his mind with whiskey. Finally, about six weeks after the death of his wife, Tom was taken aside by a long-time friend. The friend, the owner of the bank, warned Tom if he didn't straighten up and start paying attention he stood to lose his business.

Less than two weeks later, the offer Tom made to his hired helper was accepted and the feed store changed hands.

Looking like he'd aged ten years, he made arrangements with his banker friend to use the money to support the Hodges' household. He explained to his girls that he had to get away. Lizzie was at school when Hester saw her father off at the railroad station. The last she saw of him was through a window of the rail car, taking a long drink from a bottle.

# CHAPTER 21

Tom hadn't paid any attention to where the train was headed, not even in which direction it was going. It so happened that the train was west bound and upon reaching the end of the track he found himself joining a wagon trail headed for the gold fields of California.

He hadn't contacted his girls since that morning, but that was about to change. One of the things he'd been working on had been a letter. He'd started more than one but had only completed the one he carried into town. It hadn't been an easy thing to do. He didn't know what to expect their reaction would be. The sale of the store should have made their lives fairly comfortable but his disappearing like that, no telling what damage that had done.

Now, passing by the alley next to the general store made him think of Dan. His shooting the robber had saved his life, but it had also made the boy realize that his fears about the stagecoach robbery and running out on someone else's horses were groundless. At least it seemed so. Funny how things worked out.

The first thing he did was ride around to the stable and care for his horses. He was coming around and about to go into the store when he glanced up the street. Two men, plainly deep in conversation, were walking toward him on the other side. Somehow the one man seemed familiar. Instinctively Tom stepped back in the shadow at the corner of the building. When the two men passed in front of him, even from that distance he could see who they were. Ned Matlow and his ever-present sidekick, Johnny Biles.

# CHAPTER 22

Dan stood for a long minute after kicking dirt over his morning fire in preparation for beginning the day's search for the Spanish mine. Lost in thought, he stood staring off into the distance trying to remember something that would point him in the right direction. Nothing came to mind except the mental image of a pair of tall, sharply pointed peaks. Shaking his head in disgust with himself, he put a foot in the stirrup and swung into the saddle.

Stretching his body around, he let his gaze travel over the ridges he'd been travelling toward the day before. From where he sat he could see the tops of half dozen or so long, knife-edged ridges. No individual peaks.

'Well, horse, let's head a little more northerly today. Maybe from the top of that higher ridge over there we can see what we're looking for.'

Setting a heel to the animal's flank, he rode in that direction. The sun was almost overhead when, reaching a high point of land, he reined to a stop. The morning's ride had been more west than north and he figured he'd covered ten miles or so, all without spotting his mountain peaks. Discouraged, his shoulders slumping, he sat turning this way and then that, searching. Cursing silently, he was turning his body to stretch his tired back muscles when he glanced behind and saw them. Two narrow points standing high above everything.

'What the . . .' he exclaimed, turning the horse to stare. 'How the hell did I miss seeing them before?'

Letting his horse chomp at a few tuffs of grass he sat thinking about it. He finally concluded that he hadn't been looking in the right direction before and hadn't been as high up. Whatever the reason, he now knew where he was heading.

Riding steadily, he found himself dropping down into the narrow canyon later that afternoon. The shovel and gold pan were where they had left them, shoved in the crotch of one of the straggly trees growing out of a pile of tailings. After quickly hobbling his horse and tossing his bedroll next to the old fire pit, he started in on one pile. By the time it got too dark to see he had filled and washed out two pans of gravel. The gold he saw in the last of the day's light was not much bigger than grains of wheat, but spread out in the bottom of the slope-sided pan the soft glow of the material brought a real excitement to the young man.

Working from sun-up to sun-down and finding colour in almost every pan full of gravel, Dan lost track of how many days he spent. It was when the sack he was using to hold the gold couldn't hold any more that he finally decided he had enough. Breaking camp and again leaving the tools jammed in the forked tree, he mounted up and started the ride back.

'Wonder if Tom's back yet,' he said, stopping when topping out of the canyon. 'Gawd, I hope he hasn't got back and has been worrying where I was. C'mon, horse, let's get a move on.'

Having someone to worry about was a new thing. Something he found himself feeling good about.

# CHAPTER 23

The ride out of the Trinity's went quicker than the ride in; he was getting a better layout of the mountain range in his mind. Two days after leaving the Spanish workings, he was riding past one of their boundary markers and could see the upper slope they had built the soddy on. Coming closer, he watched for sign of Tom, maybe the horses. Seeing nothing, he began to wonder if he'd been mistaken in how long he'd been gone.

The door to the rough sod house was only partially closed. It looked like the wind had pushed it open just enough to let small animals find shelter inside. Tracks criss-crossing the dirt floor told the tale; field mice had taken over.

'Have to do something about that,' he said out loud, chuckling as he unpacked his saddle-bags and started a fire. Later, sitting outside enjoying a cup of strong coffee he tried to figure out how long he'd been gone. 'Well, there's nothing to do,' he finally decided, 'but to ride toward town and meet up with him.'

All the way in, Dan kept expecting to see his partner riding toward him. Coming on to the main street of Union late on the third day of riding, he was more than a little concerned. His first stop, he decided, would be the sheriff's office. There, he soon discovered, his worse fears were answered.

'Well, young man, I've been expecting you,' the rotund man said, coming up out from behind his desk to shake Dan's hand. 'Yes, sir, I figured sooner or later you'd be showing up. Sit down and get ready for bad news.'

Dan dropped into the offered chair and nodded. 'He's dead, isn't he.'

'Uh huh,' Sheriff Catlin said, settling back in his chair. 'I'm 'fraid so. It was that damn gold what done it. Just like last time, he'd just left the store after ordering a long list of supplies and was headed back to the stable. Old Watkins said he heard a shot and went to see what it was about. Found your partner lying there in the alley, his pockets all turned out. He'd been shot in the back. Didn't even have time to pull that pistol of his'n out of his pocket, neither. We buried him up in the town cemetery. I got to tell you, that plot we set aside for burying just isn't gonna be big enough.' Knowing he was talking too much, he stopped and sat watching the younger man.

'Robbed,' Dan said after as long pause. 'And I'll bet there hasn't been anyone around spending any gold, either.'

'Nope, but there wouldn't be. Not any gold like that kind you two brought in, anyhow. Watkins showed me. Pure hard rock gold, not placer. But the robber didn't get any of it. Hodges had left it with Watkins. Deposited it in his safe, you see.'

'So Tom got into town and was getting the supplies?'

'Oh, he was a busy one, that's for sure. He and I had supper over at the restaurant. First thing he done was to register that spread you two marked out. Got that all done and then mailed off a letter. Don't know who that was to, but he seemed plumb happy about it. That went out on the stage a couple days later. I wondered if I should have held it back until you came in, but decided not to. Anyway, he figured he'd be getting a load of supplies from the store and then head back out. He took a room at the hotel and was shot down the next morning.'

'I suppose like last time, nobody saw anything and the murderer hasn't been found?'

'Nope, and I talked to everyone I could find that had been in town that morning. Likely I even questioned the fella himself what did it, but didn't know it.'

Dan hung his head, not wanting the lawman to see his eyes tearing up.

'I'm going to miss that old man,' he said when he could speak. 'He and I've been through quite a lot since we met up. That's for sure.'

# CHAPTER 24

'Well, I put his horses in the corral back there by the stable and Watkins never did make up his order but it's all been paid for. I reckon now you're the full owner of that ranch. He registered it as the B-slash-H, by the way. Don't know if you knew he'd do that.'

The B-slash-H, huh? No, we hadn't talked about what to call it. The B-slash-H, a ranch with no livestock.'

'Yeah, he said something about that. There's a fella, name of Jenkins, whose got a small herd he's been trying to get shet of. I told Hodges about that and he said he'd look into it. Got Jenkins all excited, until I told him that Hodges been killed. He wants to head on over the mountains, he does. He's still got them. I'd say if you're in the market, you'd likely get a real bargain.'

Dan nodded and grimaced. 'That letter was to his family. He had two daughters back east somewhere. I guess they're my partners now.'

'You got their address?'

'Yeah. Tom spent a lot of time writing that letter. He wrote it a couple times, making changes, until he figured he got it just right. I found one of the early ones and put it in my saddle-bags before coming into town. Guess I had a feeling.'

'Well, I've heard of things like that happening. Uh huh.'

'I thank you, Sheriff,' Dan said, standing up and moving toward the door, 'for taking care of things. I guess I'll do like Tom did and stay the night at the hotel. Probably go talk with that fella, Jenkins, tomorrow.'

'You let me know and I'll ride out with you. Show you the way. Say, you plan on getting supper, I'll go along and have coffee with you, if you don't mind.'

The two men were crossing the street when Dan saw someone he thought was familiar sitting on the bench outside the saloon. Finally putting a name to the man, he felt his stomach knot up. Being careful not to look directly at the seated man he kept his head turned away.

'Hey, Sheriff,' he said after they'd past by, 'that man sitting there on that bench, you know his name?'

'Uh huh. He's pretty new in town. Came in a few weeks ago with another gent. Funny you should ask, though. Your partner, he asked me about them, too. Yeah, says his name's Biles. A real strange looking fella, isn't he?'

Biles. Without asking, Dan knew the man he'd come into town with was Matlow. Damn, would he ever get away from that stagecoach robbery? A bigger question was when did those two come to town? Before Tom was killed? He almost stopped dead in his tracks when the next question hit him; why would they come to Union? Looking for Tom? And just maybe for him?

# CHAPTER 25

'You don't look so good, uh, Dan,' Sheriff Catlin said, holding the door to the restaurant open for him. 'Wal, I can certainly guess why, learning your partner got killed and all. Likely just hitting home, huh? You can't let it worry you, though. Life isn't for the soft or weak-hearted out here in no man's land.'

Rather than try to speak, Dan just nodded and headed for one of the empty tables. Pulling a chair out and sitting down, his internal conversation went on. No, he decided, there was no way Matlow or Biles could know where he or Tom was. Thinking about it, he couldn't come up with much of a reason for them to even want to know.

Tom had never said much about how he came to get connected with Ned Matlow or why he was willing to take part in the hold-up. Dan had always figured it was for the older man just as it was for him; a man's got to eat. And too, maybe Tom hadn't known they were going to rob the stagecoach. That wasn't likely and, not wanting to know, he'd never asked. Better to let things be.

Dan didn't sleep much that night. The mattress in the hotel room was thick and soft, probably filled with as much goose feathers as cotton, and he sunk deeply into it. For someone used to sleeping on the hard ground such softness was uncomfortable. He ended up pulling his blankets to the floor and bundling up down there.

Up before anyone else, he sat on the bench outside the saloon, waiting for the restaurant to open. Sitting where he'd seen Biles sit brought back all the fear he thought he'd gotten over. It wasn't fair, he told himself, just when things are going good for us, someone has to go and kill Tom. And now those two show up. Even if they hadn't been looking for Tom, they were the kind of men who wouldn't think twice about killing someone if there was gold involved. He'd have to ask Sheriff Catlin if they had been in town when it happened.

He didn't get a chance to mention it until after breakfast, when the lawman was taking him out to talk with Jenkins.

'Wal, I don't know when they came into town,' grumbled Sheriff Catlin. 'Don't really know when they first arrived. Just seemed to be here one morning. Just like a lot of men coming back east over the mountains. Not all of them come into town and when they do, unless they cause trouble I don't always know it.'

'Were they troublesome?'

'No, I remember seeing them because of the way that one fella looks. He's sure an ugly one, isn't he?' Not waiting for an answer, he went on. 'You've got some interest in them two. Know them, do you?'

Dan didn't know how to answer that and paused before simply saying they reminded him of someone he saw back in the gold country.

They rode the rest of the way in silence. Dan may not have been talking much, but he was thinking pretty hard. Worrying.

# CHAPTER 26

The little jag of beef Jenkins was selling consisted of four bulls and eleven cows. The cattle were grouped in a makeshift corral. Two men were sitting on their heels when Dan and the sheriff rode up. The older of the two stood up slowly and was introduced as Aaron Jenkins. He was a little older than Dan expected. Probably, he figured, because the man was wearing bib overalls like his pa always wore.

'This here's my hired hand, Tony,' said Jenkins. 'We

97

was about to run these critters closer into town, hoping maybe to get someone interested in 'em. Was too bad about your partner getting himself killed. He talked like he wanted to buy this little bunch. I thought I was on my way, but, well, now you're here so maybe it'll work out after all.'

Dan didn't know much about cattle. Only what he'd learned at the Rafters' ranch. Back on the farm they always had a milk cow and Pa would buy a couple calves each spring to raise for butchering in the fall. Seeing the herd being held in place by a single strand of rope made him a little nervous.

'Yep,' Jenkins said after waiting for Dan to say something then giving up, 'they're all healthy. As you can see, they's all Texas Longhorn,' he said, sounding proud. 'It won't bother them none, no matter what kind of range you got. Now, that one bull there, the brindle-coloured one, he's about two years old. All the rest are older. That won't matter much to the cows, though. They'll all breed. Fact is, I wouldn't be surprised if most of them females won't be showing a good increase in the herd before many weeks.'

Dan nodded, wondering how Hodges would have dealt with this. 'Sheriff Catlin said you're anxious to be moving on. What kind of price you thinking of getting?'

'Yep, I'd sure like to go over to California and see what all the hullabaloo is about. But that don't mean I'm gonna give these critters away. No, sir. I figure to get twenty dollars a head.'

Dan, watching the cattle starting to mill around, slowly shook his head. 'Well, that lets me out. I've got more experience with horse flesh than cattle. I'm thinking maybe I'd better stick with raising what I know something about. Anyway, twenty dollars? If I want a few head, I figure I can find them a lot cheaper if I wait for one of them wagon trains to come along. Tom and I talked about it once. He was sure if we were patient we could get the start of a herd that way.'

Jenkins nodded and kicked at a clod of dirt before speaking. 'Yep, that's what I got here. Brought them up myself. Well, with Tony's help, of course. Now, well, I don't know. Don't seem like it'll be worthwhile trying to trail them up over the mountains. Tell you what, I figure I can get maybe ten dollars from the butcher in town. I'd have to sell them a few at a time and hang around another month or two or even three to get rid of all of them. I'll let you have them for, say, twelve?'

Dropping the reins of his horse, Dan stepped to one side, studying the herd. 'I left money with Watkins in at the general store this morning. That cash money would be a lot easier to carry over the mountains and you wouldn't have to wait. Best I can do, though, is,' he paused, pursed his lips and finally nodded, 'six dollars.'

The cattleman let his shoulders slump. 'Naw, I can't do that.'

Dan picked up the reins and stood by the side of his horse before turning to the other man. 'I understand,' he said, smiling and holding out a hand. 'No hard feelings. Sheriff, looks like I took up your morning for nothing.'

'Aw, hell,' Jenkins said quickly, 'you make it eight dollars and we deal.'

Dan stepped back and put out his hand. 'Eight dollars it is and I thank you.'

'Dammit, if'n I was younger I'd file on some land and raise my own herd, but you got a good deal, young man, and don't you forget it.'

'Well, you come on into town and I'll pay you. Even buy you a drink at the saloon.'

'I thank you and I'll be there. But I don't drink liquor, so I'll pass on that.'

Dan had been watching Jenkins' hired hand and now went over to stand beside him. 'You think I paid too much?' he asked softly.

'Uh, no. Just about what they're worth right here and now. The old man wants to go on. The question is, what are you going to do with them now that you got them?'

'Move them on to the range my partner and I filed on. What would it cost me to hire you to help?'

'You filed on range land?'

Dan nodded.

'Got water?'

Another nod.

'How much land you stake out?'

'Tom figured we got close to a thousand acres. The northern part of a valley about three days ride north and a little east of here.'

'I'll help you move the herd for five dollars a day and found.'

'That sounds good to me. After I pay Mr Jenkins off and get the packhorse loaded I'll come back out.'

'Well, me'n these critters'll be here. Make sure you got lots of coffee. I do like my coffee in the morning.'

Riding back into town, Dan decided he was lucky that Jenkins didn't drink. He would get his supplies and get out of town before evening. Going into the saloon might have meant running into Matlow or Biles. It was not likely they would remember him but he didn't want to take the chance. They didn't strike him as being the kind of men who would hang around a little town like Union and maybe they'd move on. At least he could hope they would.

# CHAPTER 27

It took the two men more than twice as long to push the herd on to B/H range as it did for Dan to make the trip in. Tony more than earned his money, Dan figured. Being the better rider and knowing more about how to push the small bunch, each day he took the drag position.

'Well, hell,' Tony had said that first morning, 'you know where we're going, don't ya? I don't. Now with a big herd, riding drag would mean eating a lot of dust thrown up by the critters, but with this little bunch it won't be no problem. You lead them out, I'll bring 'em along.'

Keeping an eye on his stock, Dan soon understood that Tony was right. The cowboy knew how hard he could move them along and he seemed to be able to sense when one or another of the contrary beasts would want to break from the others. Tony wasn't any older than Dan, but when it came to cattle he was a lot smarter.

The only thing Dan had to do all day long was make

sure he didn't get too far ahead of the bunch following along. Tony kept them moving, but also allowed them to chomp at the grass while they ambled along. During a midday break, the cowboy talked a little about the drive.

'You can move cows along pretty good but if they don't have a chance to feed you won't have much at the end of the trip. The other thing is they're better off if they get a break every four or five hours. Gives the grass they been eating time to settle down. You know, a lot like you or me when we've had a big supper.'

That made sense to Dan, although he was some anxious to get the herd on his own grass. They had made up a little campfire, boiled the coffee pot and were relaxing with a cup of the strong, black brew.

'You don't mind my asking,' Tony said, after a pause, 'what plans are you working on for these critters?'

'Well, that's something Tom and I had talked about. He figured we could start out with whatever cattle we could find and let the herd grow a bit before trying to market any of them. He'd come west over the Oregon Trail. The group he was with broke off north, there at Fort Hall. He ended up with a bunch going on toward California.

'There's another Army fort a bit south of here, Camp McGerry it's called. Tom thought if we could have a dozen or so head in two years or so we should have enough to take to McGerry. Keeping back the best and letting them reproduce, we should be able to make a drive up to Fort Hall in about five years. From then on that'd be what we'd do. I suppose that's what I'll try to do.'

Tony nodded but didn't make any comment. Dan

noted his new hired hand was a thinking man. It was clear, along with his coffee, he liked to study on something before talking about it.

# CHAPTER 28

Dan felt a lot better when they passed the rock cairn that he and Tom had put up marking the southern boundary. Even taking it easy, they had reached his own spread late in the morning of the sixth day out of Union.

'Hey, Tony,' Dan called, riding back and coming alongside the man, 'that's the marker of our range. The hill I plan on building a cabin on is a couple more miles or so on. We'll be coming up to the river before that. I'd like to keep the cattle on the other side, up closer to where I'll be living.'

'How far to this river of yours?'

'Oh, a mile, I reckon. I figure we can be far enough to let them fend for themselves before dark. The soddy Tom and I built isn't much but it's got a good fireplace. It'll be more comfortable than another night around a campfire.'

The sun hadn't dropped fully behind the mountains to the west when they stopped pushing the small herd. Getting to the soddy, after unloading the packhorse, the two men rolled their bedding out on the rope-sprung beds that lined two of the walls. Dan felt extra good knowing the beginnings of his herd was out there eating grass on his range.

'There's a creek that runs down behind the cabin,' he said, grabbing a ratty piece of toweling. 'Tom and I dug out a pretty good sized hole, big enough to bathe in. I don't know about you, but I'm getting tired of smelling myself.'

After passing a bar of hard lye soap back and forth, they sat back neck deep in the water. Dusk had settled in and Dan, looking up at the sky, could see the night's first stars.

Tony, sitting across the little pond, broke the silence. 'That range you marked out looks pretty good. How far on north do you have?'

'We're a bit over half way. In that direction,' Dan pointed east toward the ridge of another lower line of mountains, 'we're about five miles. That jagged horizon you can just barely make out is the boundary.'

The other man was silent for a while.

'All right,' he said finally, 'I've got a proposal to make. You said you'd pay me five dollars a day. Well, I don't know how long you can afford to do that, but it's awfully clear you're going to need a lot of help. Face it, there's a whole lot you don't know about raising cattle. Can't just turn them out and expect them to grow into a marketable herd. You only got four bulls out there. Something you might think about, to help your finances, is to cut out the oldest one and run it into the butcher there in Union. Won't be long and it'll be heavy. Probably bring a good bit of money. Building up your herd is going to take some time. I figure you'll need me around at least through winter.'

'Yeah, I've been thinking about that. Mr Watkins there in the general store, he's got my account. If you are to stay, say, three months, there won't be anything left in that account. I haven't come up with a way around it, but I'm working on it.'

He didn't want to say anything about the Spanish workings. After panning out the gravel from that last pile of tailings, Dan didn't think there'd be too much more to go after.

'Well, see what you think about this. You sign that strip of land from your southern marker to that little river over to me. I figure that'll give me a couple hundred acres. Now, the way you have it planned, it won't be long and there could be a small herd to send down to sell to the soldiers at Camp McGerry. Here's my idea. If you've got, say half a dozen head, you give me one of them. If there's a dozen, I'll take two. Now those animals will become the start of my herd. In the five years or so you're guessing it'll take for you to build up a sizable herd, I can have a good start on my own. And all the time, I'll be here working on your spread, showing you things you're going to need to know.'

Dan slowly nodded. 'Now that might be something to think about. Let's get some supper on the table.'

Having someone who knew what he was doing was good, Dan thought. Without having Tom around, it'd likely get lonely out so far from everything. That gave him a lot to think about.

# CHAPTER 29

Having reached an agreement, the two men started to get things going. While Dan was cutting and dragging pine logs from the upper foothills, Tony cut and dragged down slender poles and started constructing a larger corral. One side of it he screened using the longer thinner poles.

'Those mountains up there will give some protection from any northerlies but I reckon there'll be a few late calves being born and building something to protect them will be important,' he explained.

Dan wasn't sure what exactly he was talking about but didn't ask. He was too busy piling up logs for the cabin he planned on building.

Usually a few of the cows could be seen from the hillside the soddy was built into. Cattle, Tony had explained, were social animals and liked to stay somewhat close to people if they could. Deciding he hadn't seen the entire bunch recently, instead of going up to cut another log or two, he headed out in a wide circle, counting what he found. Coming in later that day he was in some panic.

'Tony, we're missing four head. I found the bulls and most of the cows, but there are four just not out there.'

The cowboy chuckled. 'Uh huh, I wouldn't be surprised. Mama Longhorns like to go off and be by themselves when they're about to give birth. I've been keeping an eye on 'em. You watch, by the time we run one of those bulls back into Union, you'll have a couple or three calves out there on the grass. That's your herd abuilding.'

They put off taking one of the older bulls to Union for two months. Tony wanted to finish his work on the corral and Dan was happy to be pulling logs down for the cabin. Both men took a few days to cut the tall grass down in one meadow. After laying it out to dry in the sun, they filled the lean-to barn with the hay to feed during winter.

Tony picked out the oldest bull; with the two of them herding the animal along they were able to maintain a steady pace and were in Union in three days. They were about an hour or so out of town when Dan thought about running into Matlow or Biles. Unconsciously he started slowing down as they got closer. Tony noticed it but didn't say anything.

After leaving the bull in the corral behind the stable, Dan went around and into the store. Tony, saying he wanted a drink, headed for the saloon next door.

Dan didn't have to touch the money resting in his account, as the price he got from Watkins for the bull paid for his list of supplies. He was out front of the store tying off that load on the back of the packhorse when he saw Matlow and Biles come out of a building across the street. Ducking his head down, he was finishing up when Sheriff Catlin came out of his office and seeing the young man called out.

'Hey, there, Bartlett. You wasn't gonna leave town without stopping by now were you?' he laughed as he strode down the street.

Dan didn't answer until he was shaking hands with the lawman, careful to keep his back turned to the two men standing on the boardwalk across the street. Just seeing those two made him feel all sweaty.

107

'Good seeing you,' Catlin said, then stepped back a bit. 'You're all pale, not feeling good?'

'Naw, I'm all right,' Dan said quickly. He wanted to ask about the two men across the street but didn't. It was quite possible that Matlow wouldn't remember him but making the sheriff curious wouldn't be a good idea. 'I guess I'm just a bit tired. It's a long ride in, you know.'

'I ran into that other one, Tony? He said the two of you have made a deal that'll give both of you some kind of cattle outfits. I've heard there's plenty of good grass land out there and it'd be good for the town if others was to follow your trail.'

While the two men stood talking, Dan kept an eye on Matlow and his partner, careful not to let the sheriff know he was.

'Come on, I'll buy you a drink,' said Catlin after a few minutes.

Rather than stay out in the street, Dan nodded and, looping the packhorse's halter rope over a railing, followed the sheriff into the saloon. Not wanting to look back, Dan could only hope Matlow wouldn't decide to have a drink too.

# CHAPTER 30

There had been no sign of either man when they left town and it didn't take long for Dan to relax once again. Although Watkins said he'd take another beef whenever they wanted to bring one in, Dan had made no promises. He figured here was enough money on the books to pay for supplies through the rest of the year and having more than one bull seemed like a good idea.

The ride back was done leisurely but both men were glad when it was over. Dan quickly got back to cutting pine logs while Tony, using the heavier packhorse, dragged them back to the hill. Both men were standing by the pile that had built up, talking about finally getting busy to starting to build when they saw riders coming in.

'Looks like four of them,' said Tony, shading his eyes with one hand, 'and I think one of them's a woman. She's riding sidesaddle. They've got two packhorses. I'll bet one of them is loaded down with extra stuff for the woman. Women are like that, you know.'

Dan chuckled but didn't say anything. These would be the first people to come visiting and he was curious about what they were looking for. Nothing else was said as the group headed directly toward them.

'Damn,' Tony said as they came closer, 'that other one's a woman, too. Riding like a man, probably wearing one of them split skirts. Yep, she's a woman all right.'

'You've got better eyesight than I have,' Dan started to say, then stopped. The riders were close enough that he could recognize the two men riding out front. Matlow and Biles.

'Damn,' he said, echoing Tony's remark. 'I don't like this.'

'Why? What's wrong?' he asked. 'You know them?'

'Yeah. Those two men. I recognize them from before. Back when Tom and I were over in California. They were bad news then and I doubt that's changed much.'

Tony didn't say anything but, pulling off the heavy leather gloves he'd been wearing, he walked over to the soddy and dropped them on the bench outside the door. Stepping inside for an instant he came back out into the sunshine wrapping his gun belt around his waist.

Dan stood waiting until the riders came up, stopping a short distance away. Watching Matlow take his time to give the place a good looking-over, studying both men and the pile of logs. Biles, Dan saw, was sitting slumped in his saddle, staring at Tony. The two women sat still for a moment, then the one sitting on the sidesaddle swung down.

'We're looking for the B-slash-H ranch,' she said briskly. 'The sheriff back in Union said it was out here somewhere.'

Nodding, Dan took his time answering. 'You've found it. I'm Dan Bartlett and you're on the B-slash-H spread.'

Looking toward the soddy, the woman frowned and turned to speak to the other woman. 'Doesn't look like much of a ranch, does it. Not like I expected, anyhow.' Turning back to look Dan over, she let the frown grow, her lips lifting with scorn. 'Well, that can't be helped, I suppose. I'm Hester Hodges, that's my sister Lizzie. We're Tom Hodges' daughters.'

It was the last thing Dan expected. Instantly his mind was filled with questions, the main one being what the hell were they doing riding with Matlow? He didn't ask any of them though.

'Well,' he said after a long moment, 'I guess that means we're partners.'

# CHAPTER 31

Hester knew the letter from her father couldn't have come at a better time. She hadn't told Lizzie, but the money they'd been living on was nearly gone. Things had changed a lot in Zebulon and, for the two women, not for the better. The friendly banker who had been entrusted with the money from the sale of the feed store had died. Hester was convinced the man replacing him had mismanaged what was left. The house they lived in going to have to be sold and the two were about to be put out on to the street. Hester was still very angry with her father, but she had to admit, his letter was a godsend.

Actually, what he had written hadn't explained much other than to say he and a young man named Daniel Bartlett had gone into a partnership. They had left the California gold country and were setting up a cattle ranch outside the town of Union in the Nevada Territory. Neither of the two men, her father said, had struck it rich in California, but had discovered a Spanish gold mine in the mountains above the ranch. The news that her father was partner in a gold mine solved everything.

Since their mother died, and especially after their father had left, Hester had seen her duty and done it doggedly. It was up to her, she thought, to make sure Elizabeth was taken care of. After all, from the moment little Lizzie was born, that was what was important. As the girls grew up, Hester's life focused more and more on her sister, making sure she was well fed and happy. With the money gone and no way to replace it, she was starting to get desperate. Then the letter came; the answer to everything.

Lizzie hadn't reacted well to the news that they would be selling the house and moving out west.

'But Hester,' she'd said when Hester tried to explain the situation, 'I don't want to leave Zebulon. All my friends are here. I'm sure Blake Carter is going to propose to me. He's been very nice to me recently, and he is so handsome. Don't you think he is, Hester? I'll just die if you make us leave.'

Blake Carter was another reason for them to catch the train to Independence, Missouri, a world away to Lizzie's thinking. Brought up in a wealthy family, the Carters owned one of the largest tobacco farms in the county. Young Blake's main interest was horse racing. He was not, as far as Hester was concerned, proper husband material. Not for little Lizzie, at any rate.

Elizabeth Hodges had grown up to be everything her older sister was not. Where Hester was built like her mother, stocky and full-bodied, Lizzie was slender. Hester's brown hair, which she kept cut short, was lifeless while the highlights in Lizzie's reddish-blonde locks sparkled in the sunshine. Lizzie's smile would light up the room. Hester's frown-wrinkled forehead made one expect storm clouds. Blake Carter may or may not propose marriage to Lizzie; no man had ever come close to even holding Hester's hand.

Selling the house on Greenwood Street was done quickly and train tickets were purchased. For the first few days of travel, first by train and then stagecoach, Lizzie sat quietly, not speaking or showing any of the excitement her sister was feeling. A gold mine. That could be the beginning of a new life for both of them. With the kind of riches a gold mine meant they could go anywhere, become new people. Well-dressed women of leisure. Being an heiress, especially of something as exotic as a Spanish gold mine, would certainly attract men. Being an old maid wasn't what Hester wanted and she wasn't getting any younger.

The many days travel on the stage was almost unbearable for Hester, but Lizzie seemed to like it. Watching through the curtained window, when the dust wasn't choking those inside, she couldn't take her eyes off the country. Long before reaching Union, Lizzie was jabbering about this strange land to anyone who would listen. On one stretch, the man sitting next to the young woman told her stories about people who came out to farm or ranch in what most easterners thought was barren wasteland.

'Indians? Not any more, there ain't,' he said, when asked about the dangers of being attacked. An older man who had obviously spent many hours in the sun and dressed in rough, worn woollen pants and shirt, dusty floppy high-topped boots with a holstered revolver belted around his waist, he knew that was what everybody wanted to hear about. He loved being the centre of attention.

'Naw, once not that many years ago you'd want to be on the look-out. But since folks started heading out on the Oregon Trail, the President had the army build a string of forts. Even then, lots of the wagon trains had problems, but the US Army's been too much for the redskins. Yes, sirree, Bob.'

'How come we don't see any farms or ranches?' Lizzie asked at one point. Hester had been very careful when there were men around; her sister was attractive and quite vivacious. There were always a lot of men to be seen, she'd noticed. A lot more than there were women. This old man, though, she considered safe. He had to be as old as their father. Once she thought about asking him if he had ever met Tom Hodges, but then didn't. She didn't want to have to explain why neither she nor her sister knew much about him.

'Wal, I'll tell you, young lady. There's so much land out here that nobody puts up fences. Cattle just runs wild until it comes time to round them up and drive them to market. Why we could be travelling through one of the big spreads right now and you'd never know it.'

Hester shuddered at the idea of living in a place where you couldn't see your neighbour. Her sister, on the other hand, appeared to enjoy the wide open spaces.

Arriving in Union, they soon learned of their father's death. That news struck Hester in the stomach, making her ill. She spent two days in bed, not coming out of the hotel room even for meals. Lizzie spent that time meeting some of the people in town, especially Cecil Watkins at the general store. He and Sheriff Catlin got very friendly. Learning they were Hodges' daughters, both Watkins and the sheriff went out of their way to be sociable. Most of the hours were spent sitting out on the sidewalk in front talking. The two men told her about living in this country and Lizzie talked about life back in Zebulon.

Hester's fear of being alone in this wild land eased as

she thought about the Spanish gold mine. Feeling better, she cautiously asked the hotel clerk if he knew of someone she could hire to guide her.

Knowing how dangerous it would be to even mention something like a long abandoned gold mine, she asked about hiring someone to take them out to the B-slash-H ranch.

Union being a small town, it didn't take long before everyone knew about the two women who got off the stage from the east. One of the first was Ned Matlow. He'd been sitting in the sunshine on the bench outside the saloon when the stage came down the street. His anger at the dust that was raised quickly faded when he saw the young woman climb down. Now that, he said to himself, was as fine a woman as he'd ever seen. The fact that she was followed by her mother didn't bother him. Not until he found out the other woman wasn't her mother but her older sister and that they were looking to hire a guide. He knew his luck had finally changed.

# CHAPTER 32

Dan offered the soddy to the two women, but Hester wouldn't think of it. She had the two men she'd hired to set up the tent the women had been using down closer to the creek. Matlow's tent was put up close by. Where Biles spent the night was anybody's guess. The four of them cooked their own supper over a fire built between the two tents. All that had Dan worried. It didn't look as if the partnership was going to be easily accepted by the easterners. He was worried about the two men they'd brought too.

As usual, the meal he and Tony had was quickly prepared, eaten and cleaned up. It had become a habit for them to take their last cup of coffee and sit out front. That was where they talked about the day and made plans.

'It sure doesn't look like that Hester'll be comfortable out here,' Tony said at one point. 'Ain't none of my business, but I don't think I'd trust those two she's got to guide her very far either.'

Dan sat considering whether to tell him how he came to know the two men. Deciding not to, he ended up merely nodding his agreement.

'That oldest one,' said Tony, after waiting to see what Dan would say and giving up, 'she wants to know about some gold mine. Rumour I heard in town was that you and your partner had brought in a poke or two. Again, ain't my business, but are you gonna share that with them?'

Dan chuckled and shook his head. 'I don't know, but it won't matter none. That Spanish gold mine she's so anxious about isn't much at all. What Tom and I found there was just what little bit those old explorers left behind a long time ago and that wasn't much. I figure she's got some idea that it's more than that. Hell, if it was, don't she think I'd be working it?'

'That's the way I figured it. But you know how it is, people think gold and stop being logical. That's probably what got your partner shot, someone thinking he'd made a big strike and had his pockets full. Too bad. Well,' he said, standing up and tossing the dregs from the bottom of his cup, 'it's time for me to turn in. Got those logs you cut to pull down in the morning.'

Dan sat for a while thinking about the two women, his partners. Tony was right. That one, Hester, was awfully quick to turn her nose up at things. The other one didn't say much, just sat back and let her sister handle it. Mighty pretty, though, he thought, smiling at the memory of her smile when she shook his hand.

Earlier in the day, he'd noticed a bank of clouds forming over the mountains. Now, under a mostly full moon, the sky had cleared. Walking down to the corral, he leaned against the top rail, looking out over the grassland below. Out there, out of sight in the dark, his herd was increasing. At least, that's what Tony was saying. Thinking about that brought back the question of his partners. What would it do to his long-range plans to have them involved? Should he talk to them about it and hope they saw the future as he did or what?

He had just about decided to let things work themselves out when he heard someone coming up the hill. Gawd, he muttered, turning around, I hope it isn't that Ned Matlow. It wasn't. In the weak light he saw it was one of the women.

It was the youngest one, Elizabeth.

'You don't mind if I join you, do you?' she asked stopping beside him to look out over the valley below. 'Oh, it is beautiful, isn't it?'

In the pale moonlight he could make out enough of her face to tell she was smiling. 'Yeah,' he said quietly,

117

'this country can be worth taking time to really look at. I don't think your sister sees it, though.'

'No, Hester isn't having a good time. She's never been very happy with her lot, not since Father left at least. Mother died just before that and I don't think he could handle the loss. Really, I was too young and I don't remember much about things before that. Afterward, well, Hester took care of things. We talked a little after supper. She's not too happy. I think she expected something more than what is here. Her picture of a ranch is, well, you know, a sprawling house, lots of barns and chickens in the yard. She's always been one to be easily disappointed.'

'But you're not?'

'No. I talked with a nice old man on the stagecoach and he explained a little about how hard life can be on a cattle ranch. From what little I know, you and our father haven't been here very long. Not long enough to build much more than you have, anyway. How did you and he meet, anyhow? We actually never heard about him having a partner until we got his letter.'

Dan had wondered how he would answer that question. With Matlow and Biles in the picture, he didn't want to say anything that would remind them of Gold Ridge.

'We met over in the gold fields,' he said finally. 'I had just arrived and he kinda took me under his wing, you might say. I probably would have starved to death if he hadn't. It's a hard life over there and not at all like the newspapers said it was. Finding gold doesn't happen without a lot of hard work and then you have to have a good claim. Most of the likely places are all taken. So we sort of started travelling together, working on a cattle ranch before coming back over the mountains. Tom had talked about seeing a pretty little valley when he was coming west with a wagon train. That's how we came to find this place.'

'I don't really remember him much, my father. What I can is seeing him working in the feed store. Not on a ranch or with cattle. It's funny to hear you talking about him.'

'He was a good man, at least to me. Always showing me things he knew about. Well, whatever we were doing. I've been lucky that way. I grew up on a farm and that's about all I know. Your pa taught me a lot of things. Now that's what Tony is doing. He's a real cowboy.'

'Does he work for you?'

'Well, not really. He's taken land on the other side of the river and is going to start a herd down there.'

'Is that what you're doing, starting a herd here?'

'Yep,' he tried not to sound as pleased as he felt over her interest. 'Those few head we run up here not long ago is the first of it. Of course there are more bulls in that small herd than I'll need, but Mr Watkins back at the general store said he'd buy the extra if we brought them in one at a time. I guess he'll butcher them out and sell them to the restaurant there at the hotel.'

'Sounds like a lot of hard work.'

'It will be, no question. But then back on that farm of Pa's, that was always a lot of hard work too. I reckon anything that doesn't come quick and easy happens because of the amount of hard work that goes into it. Pa always said if you want your house to last you got to build it on a strong foundation. Well, that's what I plan on doing here, building to last.'

'And those logs back there, are they going to be a log cabin?' Dan nodded. 'Are you going to build it on a good foundation?'

He nodded again.

'Where will it be?'

'I want to build it over there, closer to the top of this hill.'

'You know how to do that?'

'Pa and I built our barn. I don't suppose it'll be much harder than that.'

'This would be a good place for your house, looking out over the valley. Are you going to have a veranda?' Before he could answer she turned to look back over toward the mountains, all a dark mass behind them. 'I'd have a veranda that I could sit on and look out over the valley and still be able to see the mountains. That would be how I'd build it.'

'Well, I don't know. Have to admit I hadn't given it a lot of thought.'

He was enjoying the talk now that the subject of her pa had ended. Hoping to hear more from her, he was disappointed when he heard someone coming. Looking over her shoulder, he saw it was Hester.

'There you are,' the older woman said, coming up to stand looking at them. 'It isn't proper for you to be out here, Lizzie. You should know better.'

'Oh, Hester, we were just talking. Dan was telling me how he and Father met.'

'We can talk about that in the morning. Come along now,' she said, sounding to Dan snippish and abrupt. 'We have a lot to talk about and the morning is soon enough.'

'Your sister is right, miss,' Dan said, cutting in before

the woman could go on. 'Being out here in the evening is not something that folks would find acceptable. Miss Hester, Elizabeth, I'll bid you a good night.' Turning, and not looking back, he walked away.

Pushing the door to the soddy closed, he was hanging up his coat and hat when he thought he heard Tony chuckle.

# CHAPTER 33

Instead of heading up to cut more trees, both men stayed close to the soddy after breakfast the next morning. Using hand axes, they were peeling the bark off the logs when the two women came walking up the hill from their camp.

'Good morning. Isn't it wonderful this morning?' Elizabeth Hodges greeted the men, a big smile lighting up her face.

Hester was more serious. 'We need to talk, Mr Bartlett. If there is some place we can sit down?'

'Well,' Tony said, laying his axe aside, 'I'll go on up and start snaking another of those logs down. Maybe take down another one or two.'

Nobody said anything while they watched him walk over to the corral and throw a saddle on one of the horses.

Dan, thinking he'd stir up the elder sister a little, smiled. 'Well, we can go on into the soddy, I guess. I can make up a pot of coffee and we can get to know one another.'

'Sitting out here in the sunshine will be better,' Hester said, still not smiling. 'Let us go over to that bench,' she said and, not waiting for an answer, strode off.

Elizabeth glanced up at Dan, smiled and followed her sister.

'And don't bother with coffee, either,' Hester called back over her shoulder. 'I haven't had a good cup of tea since I left home. Don't you people drink anything but coffee?'

'Well,' said Dan, slowly, trying not to laugh at the woman's attitude. Nope, he thought, there is no chance she'll ever be happy out here. 'I guess we drink what we can get. Not much tea gets out here. You got to remember, most everything has to be brought from back east so there are a lot of things that we don't have. Now you go on over into California, why I've heard there isn't anything you can't buy in San Francisco. Most everything you'd want comes by ship around Cape Horn.'

'Well, that's not where we are going. Fact is, I want to get things taken care of so we can head back to Zebulon as soon as possible.'

Dan, leaning against the wall, nodded. 'I don't know what you have in mind when you say take care of things, but there are a few things we do need to discuss. Your sister and I were talking last evening about the cabin I'm planning. You two are partners in this spread so I expect I'll have to build two cabins to start.'

'No,' said Hester, not bothering to look around, keeping her gaze on Dan. 'We aren't interested in any ranch. What I want to know is, how we get to the Spanish gold mine.'

Dan half expected that. He'd thought about it before

falling asleep the night before. Getting men like Matlow to bring them out, the women had to promise more than wages and for certain more than work building a cattle outfit. The story of the gold he and Tom had found was the only answer.

'Hate to tell you, but those Spaniards got all there was to get a long time ago. Tom, your pa, figured what they found wasn't more than a pocket that they dug out, not enough to go mining for.'

Hester all but stamped her foot. 'No. I won't accept that. You say we are your partners. Well, it was our father who was your so-called partner. I think you're lying about it so you can keep it all yourself. I've talked it over with Mr Matlow and he agrees. I warn you, he is strong and will make sure I get what is mine. What my father wanted me to have. Now, where is that gold mine?'

Dan was starting to shake his head when he caught movement out of the corner of his eye. Standing off to one side were Matlow and his sidekick, Biles. Both men were standing with their hands resting on their holstered revolvers.

'You heard the lady,' Matlow snarled, 'you can quit lying and start talking.'

# CHAPTER 34

The single-action Colt revolver that Dan had bought back when Tom had been attacked was on a shelf over his bed in the soddy. He'd tried to carry it by sticking it behind the belt holding up his trousers but that had proven to be uncomfortable. He was always afraid he'd drop it. Tony had warned him, telling him the best thing was to always be armed. He'd tried to convince Dan of making it a habit. 'You never know when you're going to need it.

'Most all cowboys carry a pistol,' Tony had explained, especially when they're out riding fence line or taking care of the stock. Say your horse steps in a gopher hole and breaks a leg. You can't just leave it there, suffering. Or if you come face to face with a big, mean rattlesnake. Having your revolver hanging over your bed won't help you then, now would it?'

And it had happened; he was face to face with a couple rattlesnakes.

What he needed now was to have Tony show up. He always carried his revolver, a Colt just like Dan's. The first thing he'd do after getting dressed in the morning was to buckle his gun belt around his waist. His Colt was in a leather holster, the kind the US Army soldiers had. Only Tony had cut off the flap that held the pistol in place and used a loop of twine over the rabbit-eared hammer. Dan had figured he'd look for a holster the next time he was in the general store. Until then it was safer where it was.

The best thing to do, he decided, was to ignore the two men. He looked at Hester. 'You're not going to believe anything I say, are you? All right, you want to make a trade, get yourself a piece of paper and write it out. The share of the B-slash-H that your pa left you for directions to the Spanish mine. But I gotta warn you, there's no gold there. At least not enough to worry about.'

Elizabeth had been standing off to one side listening.

Now she spoke up.

'Hester, I don't want to be part of this. Mr Bartlett told me last night that the Spaniards had taken what gold there was. A pocket, he called it. Anyway, I think we'd be better off with a ranch than any old gold mine.'

'Lizzie, you never have thought about things realistically. Every since you were a child I've had to do the thinking for both of us. Now it's time for you to face facts. We don't have a choice. That gold mine that Father told us about in his letter is the only thing that's going to save us. This ranch won't, that's for sure,' she said, waving around with one hand. 'That cave over there that your Mr Bartlett calls home is nothing more than a dirt-floored pig pen. It's certainly not a place for two city-bred young women to live in. I mean look at it, this isn't a ranch, it's simply a barren grassy valley.'

The younger sister wasn't backing down. 'Not now it isn't much, but in a few years it could be. If you want to make a deal and trade your share of that away for something that isn't anything, then you go right ahead. But make it clear, I'm not agreeing with you.'

Hester snorted and shook her head with disgust. 'Well, you've made your bed. Just remember, I'm doing what I think is best for both of us. Now, Mr Bartlett, you start thinking about those directions while I go get some stationery from my tent.'

Watching the woman stomp off down the hill, Dan glanced in Matlow's direction. With the trade a done deal, he could tell both men had relaxed. Biles, a thin sneering smile lifting his lips, let his shoulders sag but didn't take his eyes off Dan. Elizabeth waited until her sister was nearly at the tent before hurriedly following her.

125

The two women were still arguing when they came back up to where the men were standing. Hester, her stride almost militaristic, was carrying a flat brown leather pouch and was ignoring her sister as one would a yapping dog biting at a horse's hoofs.

The woman, carefully tucking her long skirt under her, sat down on the bench and, opening the lid of the pouch and using that flat surface as a writing desk, started writing.

'How does this sound, Mr Bartlett?' she asked and read what she wrote. 'I, Hester Hodges, hereby transfer my share of the B-slash-H ranch to Dan Bartlett in trade for certain valuable information. In accepting this trade, Mr Bartlett will promise not to make any further claim on anything that develops from my use of that information. Does that meet with your approval?'

Dan wanted to laugh. 'Oh, yes, I think that will do. I guarantee you; there is nothing at that so-called Spanish mine that I'll want.'

'Very well,' she said, putting her signature at the bottom of the paper. 'Now, how do we get to the mine?'

Taking the paper, he waved it to make sure the ink was dry and nodded.

'You want me to write it out for you?'

Matlow, his voice hard and demanding, cut in. 'Don't bother. Just make sure you tell it good. Me'n Johnny here, we'll find it.'

'Uh huh. OK. That mountain range back there,' Dan started, lifting his chin to point the way, 'is the Trinity Mountains. You ride south from here a few miles and you'll come to what looks like a break in the narrow ridge line. Follow that. There is a game trail that'll take you up and over that ridge. You'll be heading in a westerly direction. When you top out, start angling more north. Riding more west than north, it'll take you half a day or so. The wide canyon you'll come down on runs more pretty straight to the north. Go up the canyon. There isn't any water that I ever saw all the way up. Keep looking to the north until you see a tall needle of a mountain sticking up like a bony finger. There are two of those there, one in front of the other. Keep riding until they are equal distance apart. With one on your right and the other on your left, you'll be in front of the mouth of a narrow canyon. There's a big old pine tree off to one side. Head in and you'll be in the canyon where the mine is. That canyon starts out broad and starts to narrow down as you climb. Up to where it looks like it ends, there are a bunch of springs coming down. There's a trail that goes on up and on to a plateau but the Spaniards' workings are at the bottom. The water from the springs pool up there. The little creek that flows out disappears into the sand a few hundred yards down. It's along that creek you'll see the grinding wheel rock they used. You'll see a lot of veins of white rock marking the far wall. Their mine was at the bottom of one of those. It isn't much more than a deep hole in the wall, goes back about ten feet or so. That's it.'

Hester had listened with a strange look in her eyes. 'How long will it take to get back there?' she asked after a moment.

'Oh, I'd say it took me a good day and a half the last time I was up there. Two days at the most.'

'OK, then. Let's not waste any more time here. We can get a long way before night fall.'

Matlow was the last to leave. 'This had better be right, bucko,' he said menacingly. 'I'll be back if you've told us wrong. Count on it.'

Dan watched as they broke camp, loading up their gear and riding out. Only one person looked back, giving him a little wave. When they were out of sight, he started toward the log pile but stopped. Glancing to where they had gone, he turned back toward the soddy. Coming out a few minutes later, he tucked his Colt in his pants pocket before going over to pick up the hand axe. Uncomfortable or not, he thought it'd be a good idea to be armed. Somehow he didn't think he'd seen the last of Matlow and the rest of them.

# CHAPTER 35

Tony didn't ask about them when he finally returned, dragging another log behind his horse. Of course, he noticed the tents were gone but waited for Dan to say something. Picking up his axe, he started debarking one of the logs. At one point, when he saw Dan standing, staring off to the south, he thought Dan would start talking about what had happened but he didn't.

He also noticed the cedar handle of a Colt was sticking out of Dan's pocket. That meant to Tony that things hadn't gone smoothly. Finally he couldn't wait any more.

'Were there problems with that homely man and his

big partner this morning?'

Dan was silent for a moment, thinking about it.

'Not as much as there almost was,' he said finally. 'When that Hester woman started in on me about the Spanish mine, I told her the truth, that there isn't such a thing. Those two outlaws weren't about to accept that, though. I figured the best thing to do to go ahead, let them find out for themselves.'

'So you told them how to get there?'

'Uh huh. But I wish I hadn't. It just doesn't sit right, thinking about it all. I can't believe Ned Matlow is going to let anything slip through his fingers, especially if it's gold.'

'You never said how you come to know those two. What happened? You know them from some other place?'

Dan thought about what to say about that too, then nodded. 'Yeah, back over the mountains, in California. Both Matlow and a couple of others were known to be bad men. Certainly the kind that if you saw them coming up to your claim, you'd want to check to make sure your powder was dry. The only reason I can believe they're on this side of the mountains is that it got too hot for them over on the California side.'

'And now they're taking those two easterners off to find a gold mine. Yeah, I can see how it would bother you.'

Dan was standing again, staring off to the south.

'I don't know what kind of deal old Tom's daughters have got with Matlow, but that oldest one's sure fired after that gold. That's what worries me the most, what'll happen when they get there and find out I was right,

129

there isn't any gold.'

'That's why you've shoved that Colt in your pocket?'

'I couldn't work with it shoved under my belt. I was afraid it'd fall out. My plan was to see if Watkins has a holster the next time we go into Union. Probably a good thing I didn't have it this morning, though. Both of them were just waiting from me to tell Hester to go suck eggs. I think they want that mine as much as she does.'

'Well, we'll just have to keep a watch out for them. How long do you figure it'll take to get there, get tired and come back?'

'Oh, a couple of days at least, then a day or so hunting and pecking. A couple more days coming back. Say a week or so, anyway.'

'Too bad this isn't the right time to be taking another bull into the general store. That'd be the best place to be when they come out of those mountains you keep staring at.'

Dan picked up his axe and started on another log.

The cabin he had in mind to build would be a single room, big enough he could partition a sleeping room off with a blanket. He hadn't mentioned it to Tony, but he figured they could build a lean-to off one side, most likely against the wall with the big stone fireplace he was planning. That way Tony could have his own area and would be OK through the cold winter months. But chopping at tree bark and thinking about the cabin he'd build wasn't enough to stop him from worrying about the gold-seekers.

# CHAPTER 36

It was worse after supper. Sitting on the bench, watching the star-filled sky pass slowly overhead, he couldn't help but think about Elizabeth. It wasn't, he decided later before going to sleep, Ned Matlow or Johnny Biles that he was worrying about, and it certainly wasn't Hester. Nope, it was Elizabeth he kept thinking about, remembering talking with her out by the corral.

He didn't sleep soundly and was up before daylight.

'Looks like you're packing for a ride,' said Tony, lying under his blankets and watching Dan fill a pair of worn leather saddle-bags. 'Not thinking about riding out to see how the herd's doing, are you?'

When Dan didn't answer, he nodded. 'No, I didn't think so. Want me to go along? It might be best if you were to come up against those two.'

'I thank you, but no. I thought I'd just go along a little, keep an eye on them, not barge in. You could ride out and see if any of those mama cows made the herd bigger, though.'

'Damn, you'd better come back. We haven't put anything in writing yet about my taking some of your south range.'

'Could do it now, if you want.'

'Nope. It'll give you a good reason to hurry back in one piece.'

Dan rode out just as the sun was breaking over the

mountains to the east. He paid close attention to things as the morning colours changed so he wouldn't think about what he was doing. One man, and not someone used to gunplay at that, going out to do what? Save the women? Make sure nothing happened to Elizabeth? That didn't make sense. With or without the gold, neither she nor Hester would be staying to help build up the ranch. They were city folk, not used to the hardships of living in the west. What the hell was he doing? More importantly, what was he going to do?

Like a dog chasing a rabbit down the hole, he couldn't give it up. It was when he stopped to give his horse a breather that it hit him; he was chasing his past. Maybe that was it. He really wanted to stamp out the memories those two men caused. Could that be it? For sure, if once and for all they were gone never to show up again and he knew it to be true, wouldn't he be able to put it all behind him? There were few days he didn't turn all sweaty and clammy thinking about riding that stolen horse, getting away from the gunfire at the stage hold-up. He could still hear Tom Hodges yelling about getting hung from the nearest tree limb. And then away from that cattle ranch outside Marysville. Not only a horse thief, but people thought he helped rob his boss. Was that what he was riding out here for?

# CHAPTER 37

Since leaving Union, Hester had made sure that their tent was set up some distance away from where the two men she'd hired as guides had dropped their bedrolls. It bothered her that she and her sister were trusting everything to such men. She knew about men. All her life she'd been fighting off men, protecting Lizzie, and the girl didn't even know it.

'How many times do I have to tell you, Liz, don't look at them?' she said, sitting with her back to the campfire, slowly brushing her sister's long hair. She had read an article in a newspaper once that said if a woman brushed her hair one hundred strokes each night she could be giving her hair an inner glow. The brushing had become their night time ritual. Hester frowned. Too bad it didn't work for her hair. That stayed thin and mousy-looking. And there were those men, Ned Matlow and the ugly one, sitting on the other side. It made her shiver. But did Lizzie see it? No. Such an innocent. 'Well,' she said, trying to remember her count, 'don't be looking in that direction. All it does is making them think you're inviting them.'

'Oh, Hester, in the first place, I'm not looking at them. I was staring into the fire, that's all. And in the second place. . . .'

'You don't understand men at all. With them, there is no second place. Why the Lord only knows what trouble you'd be in if I wasn't here to watch over you.'

'That's true. You're always there. Thinking you're protecting me when really, you're smothering me.'

'Why Elizabeth Hodges, how can you say such a thing?'

'Back there at the ranch, when Mr Bartlett and I were talking, you had to come and break in. He was explaining what he had in mind, how the ranch could grow. But all you saw was that I was talking to a man.'

'Yes, because I know about how that is. As far as that being a ranch, it's nothing close to being what anyone would think was one. I called it right, a flat, dreary pasture. And that pigsty he lives in, heavens, could you see inviting anyone to visit there? If there were anyone close enough to come for a visit, that is, and there isn't.'

'Your trouble is that you're comparing everything to how it was back home. This is all brand new. I think it's exciting to be able to build something like that.'

'I certainly do think of what life was like back east. That's where we belong, not out in this wilderness. Back there where people are friendly, civilized, and . . . and clean, for heaven's sake. Do you know how long it's been since I've had a decent bath? Look at those two men over there. I hardly think either of them has put on a clean shirt since we left Union.'

'You hired them, didn't you? Were you concerned if they had clean clothes then?'

'I hired what was available. Those two were the only ones who came offering to take us out to that, that place.'

Elizabeth went back to staring into the dying fire. Arguing with her sister had never solved anything. Hester wanted to live like she thought everyone else lived. She was so busy trying to climb up that she couldn't find comfort or enjoyment in the day. That gold had become her answer to everything when there was a future in that ranch. Not wanting to think too much about the man there, she couldn't help herself. Looking up at where that Matlow and his partner were sitting, drinking from a bottle, she shuddered. They were nothing like Mr Bartlett, that was for sure.

'Hester, I wanted to ask you, how are we paying those two? Didn't you tell me that it took the last of our money to stay in that hotel as long as we did?'

The other woman fidgeted a little, angry for having lost count. This was something she didn't want to discuss. 'It doesn't matter. We'll get to the Spanish mine in another day or two and then things will be OK.'

'No, I think I should know. If we couldn't pay for the hotel room and meals in the restaurant, how are we paying for someone to guide us?'

'Well, if you must know,' having decided to restart her count at fifty, Hester went back to stroking the brush, keeping her quiet count nice and steady, 'I promised Mr Matlow a share of the gold. That was the only thing I had. He was gracious enough to agree.'

'So he is now a partner? You gave over being partners with Mr Bartlett but are continuing being a partner with him?' Elizabeth lifted her chin toward the other side of the fire. 'I for one would trust Mr Bartlett a lot more than I ever would those two.'

'That doesn't matter. What matters is with the help of Mr Matlow we will have the gold and can go back to a civilized world. I'm not happy about it but, well, we'll just have to live with it. Anyway, I don't trust them any more than I would any other man. I knew we would be at their

135

mercy when I hired them so I took special precautions. See?' Reaching into a pocket of her long wool dress she pulled out a small pistol.

'You've got a gun,' Elizabeth exclaimed. 'Where did you get that? Do you know how to use it?'

'Of course I do. Mr Watkins showed me. He loaded both barrels and showed me how to cock the hammer back and then all I have to do is touch this trigger. He said just showing someone that I had it would likely stop them in their tracks. It would show that I meant business. But if I had to shoot, he warned me to make sure they were close because it wouldn't be good if the person threatening me was very far away. He told me it would stop a man if I shot him.'

'Do you think you could do that? Shoot a man, I mean?'

'Certainly, if I had to. Just point it and pull the trigger. It's a derringer, Mr Watkins said. And the bullet is a 40, whatever that means. He gave me half a dozen of them. Now, if either of those two men, or anyone else for that matter, causes you or me any trouble they'll find out if I paid attention to the storekeeper. And stop looking at me like that. I'm not a fool. I realize we are all alone out here with two very unsavoury men, but if that's what it takes, then, well, there's nothing we can do about it.'

'Hester, sometimes you amaze me. However, I suppose you're right, we've made our bed and now we must live with it. I just hope that what you've done works out for the better. Now, I'm going to bed. I've had about enough of this day.'

For a long time after her sister had gone into their tent, Hester Hodges remained by the fire, brushing her hair and thinking about what the future would be like. What it had to be like. There was no other future possible without that gold mine.

# CHAPTER 38

Dan was up early the next morning, had drunk a cup of hastily brewed coffee and was in the saddle as the sun came up. Feeling the warmth on his back, he followed the wide canyon, keeping one eye on the mountain tops ahead and the other on the trail left by the group he was following.

Riding with the women, he figured Matlow would be travelling a lot slower. For certain Hester especially would be hard to hurry. She wanted the gold mine real bad but there was something about her that made him think even with that pushing her, she'd not be rushed.

'Well, horse, from what I can tell, they're moving right along. I expect we'll catch up before they reach the twin peaks and the narrow canyon. What do you say, am I right?' As usual, the horse didn't even twitch an ear.

The horse, one of the two he and Tom had traded the two stolen horses for, had a good bit of mustang blood and was a hard worker. That was something that Tony had told him about, how some horses were better with cattle than others.

Dan didn't want to think about the two horses. They were the ones he and Tom had ridden away from the

Rafter ranch on and that was a time he didn't want to think about. But now, riding on the back of one of them, he was glad he had such a good horse.

He didn't push too hard that day, not wanting to get too close to Matlow and the women. He figured he'd have a hard time explaining why he was there, if they found out he was following them. Along about mid day he finally saw one of the needle topped mountains off to the north. From what he could recall, he should be able to reach the canyon with the Spanish mine in it with another half day of riding. He'd have to start thinking about what he'd do then.

# CHAPTER 39

Hester's party reached the narrow canyon late on the second day. To the disgust of the two men supposedly guiding the women, she wasn't about to be hurried. When she had hired the horses from the stable, she had requested a side saddle for both of them. Elizabeth wouldn't hear of it.

'I never used a side saddle when we were back in Zebulon,' she said, shaking her head, 'and there's no reason to start now. I've got my split skirt and I can sit a saddle as well as the next person. Those side saddles aren't comfortable and you know it.'

Taking her sister aside, Hester angrily explained her

reasoning. 'Don't you understand? These people think we're nothing more than weak Nellie easterners. Weak women. Now if they want to think that, then good. It'll make them want to take care of us. Anyway, I don't think it's lady-like for a woman to ride like that, astride a horse. I want the people out here to know that we are ladies, not a pair of strumpets. But I won't argue with you. If you don't care what people think, then far be it for me to fight you over it.'

'No,' responded the younger woman realistically, 'I really don't care. What I do care about is the fact that we'll be doing more riding than either of us are used to. I'm thinking more about my comfort than about appearances.'

Hester never complained, but she demanded they stop every so often and that slowed things down. The sun had gone behind the mountains behind them when Matlow decided the open place in the hills to the right was the mouth of the canyon they were looking for. The pine tree off to one side was just about like that fool had described.

Riding a way into the narrow canyon, Hester decided it was too late in the day to ride any further.

'It'll be a lot easier to find what we're looking for in the morning, with the full daylight.'

Johnny snorted but didn't say anything. Matlow simply nodded and started looking for a good place to make camp. While the two women were setting up their tent, the men stripped the gear off the horses, gave them a quick brush down and went off to find firewood.

'How much longer we gonna put up with that woman?' whined Johnny once they got far enough away. 'For Gawd's sake, we coulda been here yesterday if she'd get her butt going. We don't need her any more anyhow.

The gold mine has got to be up that way, doesn't it?'

'Dammit Johnny, there you go, always getting in a rush and not thinking things through. Yeah, I agree with you. She is holding everything up. But what's the big hurry? It ain't like you got someplace you gotta go, is it? So stop your stewing. Another day or so and we'll find out if there's any gold at that mine. I kinda doubt there is. Or not much anyhow. You don't think that fool back there would be working to build up a ranch if he knew where there was a gold mine, do you? Not on your tin type. And don't be so quick to want to get rid of that one. Didn't I tell you? After we get want we want, she's all yours.'

Johhny Biles started picking up an armful of dry tree limbs from around the big pine tree, thinking about what Matlow had said.

'Yeah, but that ain't the one I want,' he said, finally. 'And I ain't so quick to think there's no gold. That kid wants to have a ranch. He got the land and a few head and he paid for it with gold, didn't he? Uh huh. So there has to be gold there someplace. I'll wait. It'll be worth it.'

Carrying as much firewood as they could, the two started back. Matlow stopped before they got too close and glared at his partner.

'You pay some mind to what I say, Johnny. I mean for this to go just like I plan.'

'All right, Ned, I still don't think it's fair, but you're the boss. C'mon, I'm hungry.'

The last of the whiskey they had brought was gone, so after eating the meal prepared by Hester and Lizzie, the two men turned in. After cleaning up the pots and pans, using sand in place of water to scour them, and with the sound of one of the men's snoring, the women went into their tent.

'Now that's one thing I'll be glad when it's over,' murmured Hester, sitting up slowly brushing her hair, carefully counting to herself. 'That snoring. Oh, to get a good night's sleep in a proper bed after a long hot bath, that's what I'm dreaming about.'

'I like the idea of a hot bath,' said Elizabeth quietly, 'and enough hot water to properly wash up those dishes.'

'Well, you think about that, young woman. That's what life would be like for any wife of a rancher out here. It's not a bit like the civilized world we'll have after we get that Spanish gold.'

Elizabeth didn't comment but rolled into her blanket. She closed her eyes thinking about Dan Bartlett and his ranch.

On the other side of the campfire, Ned Matlow was laying back listening to his partner's snoring and smoking his last cigarette of the day. He'd been lying there since Biles had gone to sleep, thinking about what Johnny had said.

Finally he nudged the man awake and growled in his ear. 'You listen to me, Johnny, don't you go getting anxious. You've got a bad habit of getting ahead of yourself. Letting those two ride along peaceful is a lot easier than trying to force them to go. And you can forget about the young one. She's mine. We'll split whatever gold we find or whatever money they may be carrying, but that Lizzie is all mine.'

'Dammit. . . .' Biles, slow to come awake, started to argue but stopped when he heard the warning in Matlow's words.

# CHAPTER 40

Dan spent a restless night, tossing and turning. At first he tried to tell himself it was that he'd dropped his bedroll on an especially rocky place. Sometime late, well after the moon came up, now at its fullest and lighting up the hillside and the surrounding landscape almost as if it were an overcast day, he gave up. Kicking the coals from his supper fire and tossing on a few pieces of dry brush, he heated up the leftover coffee.

Maybe that was it. The bright moonlight was keeping him awake. Standing, his bare toes digging into a sandy spot, he had to shake his head. Naw. That wasn't it. He was worried about the women.

'No,' he said, almost in answer to the howl of a coyote off in the distance, 'it isn't the women, it's just one of them. Elizabeth. And that's foolish of me. All we did was talk a few minutes there by the corral. Now here I am mooning like a lovesick calf. C'mon, Daniel, get serious. She likely hasn't given you any thought at all.'

Sitting back down on his blankets, leaning back against his saddle, he tried to think it through. Elizabeth, unlike her sister, wasn't so all-fired interested in the Spanish gold. Hadn't she been interested in what he'd been telling her about his plans for the ranch? Sooner or later, he'd have to find a wife. That only made sense. But Elizabeth? Would she make a good rancher's wife? She was young and strong, but she was used to life back east,

142

with wide sidewalks where people could stop and talk while doing their shopping. Yeah, and more than the few people that Union boasted to be talking with. It'd be a big change for her.

What would happen if it got too tough for her, living in the soddy until he could get the log cabin built. What would she think, having to pack water from the creek until he could get a well dug. Maybe it would be better if he just forgot her. Let her and her bossy sister find out there wasn't any gold and they'd have to go home. She would still be his partner. Fact is, he'd halfway decided he wouldn't honour that quit claim her sister had signed after all. It was all foolishness. He could work out something. Maybe send them money once the herd was built up and the place was showing a profit.

It would be profitable, too. Sooner or later. Wasn't it Hodges who'd told him that it wouldn't be long before California was made a state? That would mean a lot more easterners moving west. The US Army would have to protect these settlers and they'd need beef. That's what would make the B-slash-H ranch profitable.

That would be the best thing for him. Stop mooning over Hodges' youngest daughter and go back to the ranch. There was too much work to get done before winter set in to be lollygagging around, following Matlow's group, sticking his nose in where it didn't belong.

Tossing the cold coffee dregs out and banking the campfire once again, he crawled back into his blankets. He'd head back in the morning. With that decision made, he was able to fall asleep.

# CHAPTER 41

The four riding toward the Spanish gold mine got a late start the next morning. Over night the sky had turned overcast and by the time they got the morning coffee brewing it had started raining. Not a hard rain, but one the Indians called a Woman Rain, soft and gentle, the kind that would soak in and bring the wild flowers to bloom.

Hester was the first to complain. 'There's no reason to hurry this morning that I can see,' she told Ned Matlow. 'If you have us in the right place we should be within a few hours ride to the Spanish mine. We're in the desert, for God's sake. This shower can't last long and there's no reason for us be getting all wet and soggy. For sure the mine isn't going anywhere.'

Biles didn't hide his anger at the woman. He'd woken up thinking about what his partner had said, the young one was not to be touched. Dammit, he wanted to scream, we're partners, ain't we? Now that surly broad wanted to sit around all day. It wouldn't be so bad if we'd brought another bottle or two. Steaming, he started to tell the cow to get her gear together or get left behind when Matlow caught his eye, shaking his head.

'Well, I guess it wouldn't matter much,' he said calmly, sitting back and reaching to put the fire-blackened coffee pot closer to the heat. 'From what that young fool rancher said, I figure we'll be making camp tonight right at the mine or awfully close to it. He said there was a

144

small creek there, didn't he? Probably a good place to set up for a few days to see what is there.'

Biles didn't so much as glance at Matlow when told to go round up an armload of firewood. Somehow, he told himself as he stomped away from the fire, he was going to get what he wanted. And that didn't mean that snivelling woman. She should have stayed back east and let people out here get on with things.

The rain didn't last long and they were loaded up and on the move within an hour or so. Other than irritate Biles, the storm had little impact on anything. The storm clouds quickly disappeared and the sun came out, warming everything up. Soon, with the exception of small clumps of pale yellow flowers, there was little sign that it had even rained. Elizabeth thought the flowers looked like miniature daisies. She wanted to stop and pick some, but didn't suggest it after noticing the black looks passing between the two men.

Hester might have felt confident that she could protect them, but Elizabeth wasn't so sure. Since learning about the little pistol that her sister carried, she'd noticed how Hester always kept one hand in her pocket. Maybe, Elizabeth thought, Hester didn't feel so sure about things after all. She wished she'd argued more about making this trip.

Matlow, not wanting to give Johnny an opportunity to complain, rode ahead and was the first to see the little creek.

'Hey,' he called back, 'we're there.'

Standing tall in the stirrups, he waved and pointed to the far wall of the ravine they had been riding through. 'This has got to be it. There's those streaks of white

145

quartz that rancher told us about. See?'

At mention of the rancher, Elizabeth felt a stab in her chest. I wish, she said silently, that he was here now. I'd feel safe then. But he wasn't and all she could do was nudge her horse a little so to keep up with Hester.

Hester, hearing the man's call and seeing the faint white marks looking like thin waterfalls flowing down the far side, had forgotten all about her fears. The gold mine had to be close by. Excited, she moved her body, urging her horse to move faster.

It was a lot like Mr Bartlett had described it. A small pond with the creek flowing on down the narrow canyon. Hester's horse had stopped next to the one Matlow had been riding. She was out of the saddle and hurrying to where the big man was standing, looking at a rough wide stone wheel. It had to be that grinding wheel that the Spaniards had used. Hester felt like laughing out loud.

Biles remained sitting on his horse. He'd watched Ned climb out of the saddle and walk over to the round rock, followed by that bossy woman. Well, so there was supposed to be a gold mine here, was there? Looking around he disgustedly shook his head. Didn't look much like any gold diggings he'd ever seen. Well, maybe that's all right, too. Get this thing over with so they could move on. There had never been a good enough reason to be traipsing around with these two women anyhow. If they were packing any money or anything worthwhile, he didn't see it. If there was, he couldn't see why they didn't just take it once they got away from Union. There might be something worthwhile in it, Ned had said. Biles snorted. Spanish gold mines. Well, where was it? No gold? Then that only left one thing for the two men and dammit, he knew which one he wanted.

# CHAPTER 42

'Look there,' said Hester excitedly, coming back to the horses, still feeling the first rush of exhilaration. Standing next to Elizabeth, she pointed toward a straggly looking tree. 'There's that shovel Bartlett said he'd stuck in a tree. This is the place. The gold mine is here, Elizabeth. We've found it. Now you'll see.'

Ned Matlow, walking a short way away from the arrastra, stopped to study the far wall before coming back to where the others were.

'I figure we'll be here a couple days,' he said. 'Once we find where those Spaniards were digging it'll take some work to see if there's anything there. We'll set up our camp there close to the pond. That little piece of grass will keep the horses satisfied. It's still early enough in the day so Johnny and I can take a look along that wall over there. I reckon that'd most likely be where any mining would be done. C'mon, Johnny, let's strip the gear off these horses.'

After the two men had left them, Hester and Elizabeth started setting up their tent. Hester wasn't much help, looking up time after time in the direction the men had gone off.

'I wonder what's keeping them,' she said after a while. 'It shouldn't be too hard to see where someone's been digging, should it?'

Elizabeth shook her head. 'Hester, think about it. Those Spanish explorers weren't here yesterday. Mr

147

Bartlett said any mining they had done would have been a long time ago. He said when they first found it that Father had said it could have been as much as a hundred years or more.'

'Blast that man. Lizzie, don't believe everything he told you. I don't like even thinking about him.'

'Is that because you're starting to feel guilty?'

'Guilty? Why in the world should I feel guilty?'

'You think we're going to find a lot of gold, don't you? And if we do, and you traded your share of the ranch, he'll be losing his share of it. I know you. You want that gold and you don't want to have to give any of it to anyone. But you're forgetting the bargain you made with Mr Matlow, aren't you? And how sure are you that those two men won't want it all for themselves? Hester, I think we may have more here than we can handle and I don't mean gold.'

Hester angrily waved her sister's comments aside and was about to say something when she heard a call. Turning, she saw Johnny Biles come through the brush that lined the creek. Standing and waiting, she shivered a bit at the sight of the misshapen man. Unconsciously her hand dropped into her pocket and gripped the handle of the derringer.

# CHAPTER 43

It didn't take long for the two men to find signs of where the Spaniards had dug into the wall of the ravine. The veins of quartz ran in broken streams of dirty white all along one stretch. Near the canyon floor, in among the loose rock and boulders, there was plenty of evidence that someone had chopped at the quartz. Ned Matlow kicked at some of the rocks in one pile before moving to the next.

'Dammit, how am I supposed to tell if there's anything there?' he asked, using the toe of his boot to shove one of the larger rocks aside.

Johnny Biles knew better than to say anything. He'd followed his partner but didn't get excited. Over in California it was the same thing. He never saw any gold in any of the creeks or streams and didn't bother looking. The only gold he thought of was what some other dirt-grubbing fool had. And all it usually took was to point his revolver at that kind of idiot to take it away from him. Oh, there'd been a few times he'd just shot the man to get his poke, but that hadn't happened often. Well, walking had never been something he liked doing in his high-heeled riding boots. As worn as they were, they were damn uncomfortable. Going along kicking at rocks made even less sense.

The two made their way along the face of the slope, stopping here and there until they found one place a little different. A couple times they had found where a hole had been dug into the rock, but only a few feet deep. Matlow was beginning to worry that this was what the Spaniards had done, simply found pockets of gold in those places and took it all. That was before they found where the hole went back a lot farther.

'You see that, Johnny, that's got to be the mine those Spaniards worked.'

Biles got close enough to look back into the darkness. 'Man, I ain't going back in there. That looks like some place there'd be rattlesnakes or who knows what.'

'Oh, Christ, there wouldn't be any snakes in there. It's likely that some animals, you know, coyotes or foxes or something, they'd use it, but not snakes. Snakes like little holes they can hide in. C'mon, let's see where it goes.'

The opening wasn't big enough to walk into. Matlow had to get down on his hands and knees to crawl in. He stopped with his body about halfway in.

'It don't go back far at all, Johnny. I can see where they stopped digging. We're going to need some light to see what they left, though,' he said, backing out.

Standing up, brushing the dirt off the knees of his pants, he nodded. 'Look, you go get the shovel that's stuck in that tree. We can use that to dig out some of what's in there. See if there's any gold. It's too dark but we can tell pretty quick if we get some of that rock back there out in the sunlight.'

Biles didn't like it much, but he'd always done what Matlow said.

Walking back up the creek, he cut through the willows growing on the banks of the water and stopped. The two women were standing next to their tent talking. One, the bossy old cow, was waving her hand, probably giving the young one a talking to. He stood too far away to hear but close enough to see, and he liked what he could see. That young one, Lizzie, was sure a looker all right.

Damn that Ned Matlow, thinking he could say who got what. There wouldn't be any gold in that hole, Johnny knew. Hell, even he knew better than that. Spaniard or not, no man's gonna just walk away if there's gold to be dug out of the rock. No, sir. And that's what they'd done, just walked away. Well, so had that fool, Hodges. He and his partner, Bartlett, hadn't they just filled a couple pokes and rode away? Not likely to do that if there was more, now, would they? Huh uh.

So, no gold. What did that leave them? Whatever those two women were packing, that's what. That and the women themselves.

Standing in the willows he thought about it and then smiled. No reason to put it off, was they? If Matlow wasn't around then there was no reason not to go ahead and take what he wanted. Yeah, and then old Ned could have what was left.

Smiling he stepped out of the willows and walked toward the women.

# CHAPTER 44

'Hester, here comes that ugly one. What do you think he wants?'

'I don't know. He's smiling and probably doesn't know that it makes him look worse.' She waited until Biles got closer. 'Where's Mr Matlow? Did you find the mine?'

Biles stopped a few feet away and for a moment stood looking the two women over, one at a time. Finally, still with the smile showing his teeth, a couple broken stubs and the others looking grey and dingy, he nodded.

'Now don't you go worrying about what we found or didn't find. That ain't what I came back for. Missy,' he said glancing at Elizabeth, 'you go on back into that tent.

151

And you,' he looked at Hester sneeringly, 'you take a walk down by that creek there and wait until I call you.'

Elizabeth didn't move. Hester did, taking a step to put herself more between them.

'What are you talking about? Where is Mr Matlow? How come you're not with him?' Taking her eyes off Biles, she craned her head around, looking past him toward the willows he'd just came out of.

'Don't you never mind about Ned,' snarled Biles. 'He's too busy digging at that so-called mine. Ain't nothing but a hole in the ground but he's all excited about it so he don't have time to worry about you. Now, beauty,' he said, raising his voice and starting to step past Hester, 'I ain't telling you again. Get in that tent. You'n me's gonna have a little fun. I been waiting for this a long time and I ain't gonna be put off. Get moving, now, you hear?'

Hester's face went white. Raising her hand she made to push against the man. 'No,' she said, as forcefully as she could, 'you stay back. Lizzie, get the axe there. Mr Biles, I'm warning you, keep away from us.'

Biles chuckled. 'You're warning me? I told Ned a long time ago to get rid of you. Ain't nothing but a meddlesome old cow anyway. Uh huh, you got just one chance to keep from getting smacked. Now get outa my way.'

Putting up his hand to push the woman aside, he was moving toward her when she pulled the derringer from her skirt pocket and without hesitating, pulled the trigger.

# CHAPTER 45

Ned Matlow sat looking into the dark mine opening, thinking about what it would mean if there did happen to be gold in there. Most likely if there was it'd be what the Spaniards had overlooked. It could have been, he was telling himself, that they were forced to leave. Say they were digging at it and a bunch of Indians came at them. There wasn't any sign of a battle but hell, that would have been years and years ago. If things got too hard, wouldn't the Spanish miners run to save their lives? And wouldn't they just carry what they could? Leaving everything else behind? Old Hodges came in packing a couple sacks of gold, hadn't he? There had to have been some left here.

Feeling like maybe his luck had finally changed, he got to his feet and, full of nervous energy, started walking back and forth. Hurry up, Johnny, he wanted to yell. How long does it take to go get that damn shovel and get back?

Matlow stopped in mid stride when the thought came to him. Picturing Johnny going back to the camp to get the shovel, and with the women there, there'd be nothing to stop Johnny from. . . .

'Oh gawd, no. That damn fool,' he said already running back toward the camp.

Running flat out, his boot came down on a rock which rolled, throwing his stride off. He fell to his knees. Slowly, painfully, he got back up and feeling like he'd twisted one ankle, waded across the creek, limping. Damn, he cursed silently, pushing through the brush in time to see Johnny push past Hester.

'No,' he called, hobbling faster, trying to stop the man from doing what it looked like he was about. 'Johnny, not now. Stop!'

The sound of the gunshot brought him to a halt. Instinctively his hand dropped to his holstered Colt as he watched Biles stagger back a few steps then fall.

Surprised, Matlow watched his partner crash to the ground. Looking up at the woman, he saw she was holding a hide-out gun, the barrel pointing in his direction. Not thinking, just reacting, he finished drawing his six-gun and bringing it up, touched the trigger. His bullet caught Hester full in the chest, knocking her back.

With a scream, Elizabeth ran to her sister's still body and threw herself down, lifting her head. 'No, Hester, no,' she didn't know she was screaming, tears cascading down her cheeks.

Hearing Matlow hobbling toward her, she screamed at him, to stay away.

'You bastard, you've killed her. You killed my sister!'

# CHAPTER 46

At the sound of gunfire, Dan drummed his heels into the horse's flank. Having made up his mind that he had no business following Matlow and the women he had turned his mount away, heading back the way he'd came. Less than a quarter of a mile on he reined in and sat for a long moment thinking.

'Dammit, horse, I can't leave those women back there with men like Ned Matlow. And that partner of his. No, we have to go back. It won't matter if I can't explain what the hell we're doing.'

Turning once again, and holding the horse to a steady trot, he wasn't too far away when he heard the two shots, the first was faint and he wasn't sure exactly what it was. A brief moment or two later, the second left no question.

Coming close he saw Matlow grabbing at Elizabeth's arm, trying to pull her away from where she was huddling next to a bundle of something on the ground. When she screamed, Dan reacted with a loud Apache-like yell. Matlow, his long-barrelled gun in one hand, the girl's arm in the other, whipped around to face the oncoming rider.

Bringing his horse to a sliding halt, Dan was out of the saddle in an instant, pulling at his own Colt .45 as he swung to the ground.

Jerking to get the revolver free from his pocket, he stopped when Matlow jammed the barrel of his pistol into Elizabeth's side.

'Leave it, cowboy,' the outlaw warned, earing back the weapon's hammer. 'You don't want the same thing to happen to this little beauty what happened to her sister, go ahead, keep clawing at that gun of yours.'

Dan froze and then slowly let go the gun butt, letting his hand fall away. Trying to make sense of what the big man had said, he glanced down, recognizing the heap of material at Elizabeth's feet was the body of her sister.

'Why'd you have to kill her?' he asked slowly. 'There isn't any gold here and if there were, it'd be hers. You'd need her.'

'Naw, I don't need anyone, least of all someone like her. Anyway I saw her standing there after she'd shot Johnny, holding her little derringer. I thought it might be a double-barrelled gun and that she was gonna get me next. Now, slowly pull that revolver of yours and toss it over there in that brush.'

Dan hesitated until Matlow jerked Elizabeth around, keeping his pistol tight against her side, her body more between the two men.

'Do it, cowboy, or do I need to plug her now?'

Again moving slowly, Dan drew the revolver from his pocket and flipped it into the low lying, spiny-looking limbs of the scrub that Matlow had indicated.

Chuckling, and pointing his gun at Dan, the outlaw released Elizabeth's arm. Freed, the girl dropped down next to her sister's body and, grasping one lifeless hand, started crying.

Without looking away from his captive, Matlow growled for her to stop the bawling.

'Dammit, if there's one thing I don't need now, it's a caterwauling female, so shut it up, you hear me?' he ordered gruffly.

'Leave her alone, Matlow. She's grieving for her sister. How'd she come to shoot your partner, anyhow?'

'Ah, hell, I don't know. He wanted this one and I told him he could have the old bag, but the young one was mine. We found the mine and he came over to get the shovel and, well, he must have thought it was his chance.' He chuckled again, 'Didn't know the cow was packing a gun or had the guts to use it. Well, he learned, didn't he?'

Using the toe of his boot, he nudged the crying girl. 'Shut it off, I said. Wailing and whining like that ain't gonna bring her back.'

'Leave her be, Matlow. She's in shock. That's her sister lying there. The only family she has. That reminds me, was it you that killed her pa?'

'Naw, it was Johnny what done that. We spotted him there in town and at first thought he'd been following us. But that didn't make any sense. Then in the saloon we heard that fat fool of a sheriff telling someone that old Tom had come in with a poke filled with gold. Well, Johnny wanted to go get him right then, but I argued against it. Maybe there'd be more than one sack of gold. But Johnny was all for killing Hodges anyhow. He blamed the old fool for running out during a stage hold-up that went bad. Hodges and some kid had been holding the horses and when the posse came riding in shooting and yelling, Johnny and me got away in the rocks. That's when we discovered Hodges and the kid had taken off on our horses. I gotta say, I thought it was funny, they had stolen our horses and run off, and we'd stolen those same horses earlier. Johnny didn't think it was funny at all.'

Dan didn't know what to say. Matlow, still laughing to himself, went on. 'You got to admit it's funny how it worked out, Johnny shoots Hester's pa and then she killed him. Now you gotta laugh over that, don't ya?'

Dan didn't think Elizabeth had been paying any attention but she had. At what she'd heard, her moaning and crying took on a new sound.

'Dammit, woman, I told you to stop that blubbering.'

'She likely can't help it,' Dan cut in quickly, 'hearing you talk like that doesn't help any. Here, I've got a bottle of brandy in my saddle-bags. A drink of that'll help her get herself past this.'

'Brandy?' said Matlow, suddenly smiling and sounding pleased. 'You got a bottle in there? Hell, yes, go ahead, dig it out. But do it slowly, I ain't trusting you.'

Turning to open the flap on the saddle-bag, Dan reached one hand in and started digging around. Glancing toward where Elizabeth knelt, his face abruptly looked shocked.

Matlow, watching Dan's movements closely, saw that look and glanced quickly down at the girl.

Seeing the gunman's eyes move, Dan grasped the butt of his pa's pepperbox pistol and without bothering to unwrap the oily rag he'd used to protect it, brought the gun around pointing at Matlow and pulled the trigger twice. The gun bucked in his hand firing once.

Quickly ripping off the rag that was jamming the barrels, keeping them from revolving and firing the second time, Dan was about to shoot again when he saw that Matlow was looking down at his chest, a surprised look on his face. Holding his fire, Dan watched as the outlaw's knees slowly buckled. Like a tree falling in the forest, the big man fell first to his knees then flat out, face in the dirt. Ned Matlow was dead.

# CHAPTER 47

Supper that evening was a quiet affair. Elizabeth sat on one side of the fire watching listlessly as Dan fried strips of thick bacon slices in a pan. When he handed her a plate of food, setting a cup of coffee on a rock nearby, she just sat, not speaking, holding the plate. After finishing his own meal and seeing that she hadn't touched her food, he went about cleaning up.

Before dark, while Elizabeth remained next to her sister, he had used one of the horses to move the bodies of the two men down to the Spaniard's mine. Putting both bodies as far back in the mine as he could, he started piling rocks in the opening, blocking it to keep out any varmints.

When the campfire had burned down, Dan got his bedroll and spread it out very near where he'd slept the first time he and Tom had spent the night there. Lying back and using his saddle for a pillow, he watched as Elizabeth gently covered her sister's body with a blanket before disappearing into her tent.

Up before the sun had come over the western lip of the ravine, Dan took the shovel and finding a grassy spot on the far side of the pool began digging a grave.

'This is a good place,' said Elizabeth, standing at the head of the grave after he'd tenderly laid the blanket wrapped body in the bottom, 'Hester meant well and to the very end she did just as she'd always done, protected me. I think it's somehow fitting that she is buried here, right next to the Spanish gold mine she wanted so desperately.'

# CHAPTER 48

Mounted and ready to head out of the ravine, they stopped to look over the area.

'It is quite beautiful, isn't it,' Elizabeth said quietly. 'Do

159

you think you'll ever come back here?'

Dan smiled a little and nodded. 'Well, probably. There are some bad memories here, but,' he pointed to the remaining piles of tailings, 'there is a bit more of the gold those Spaniards left behind and you never know, we might want to increase the herd a little quicker.'

'You said "we", didn't you.' It wasn't a question.

Dan nodded. 'Uh huh. What do you think you'll be doing, heading back east?'

'No,' she said, then looking directly at him, went on, 'there's nothing for me back there, and I believe I'm still part owner of a cattle ranch near here, aren't I?'

Dan nodded again and touched his horse's flank with a heel. Riding at a walk neither of them said anything for a long while. Finally, looking at the woman riding next to him Dan broke the silence.

'It'll be another month or so before we run another bull into Union. Do you think it'll be all right to wait until then to be looking for a preacher?'

Lizzie nodded. 'Yes. Does this mean you're going to build a long veranda on that log cabin you're planning?'

'Uh huh,' he said, a big smile creasing his face, 'and I guess we'd better build the cabin in a way we can add to it as the ranch and our family grows.'